14 DAYS

Also by Luke Short
in Large Print:

High Vermilion
Savage Range
Bought with a Gun
Stalkers
Station West
Hard Money
Barren Land Showdown
A Man Could Get Killed

This Large Print Book carries the
Seal of Approval of N.A.V.H.

The Man from Two Rivers

Luke Short

G.K. Hall & Co.
Thorndike, Maine

Published in 1996 by arrangement with Kate Hirson & Daniel Glidden.

G.K. Hall Large Print Paperback Collection.

The text of this Large Print edition is unabridged.
Other aspects of the book may vary from the original edition.

Set in 16 pt. Century Schoolbook.

Printed in the United States on permanent paper.

Library of Congress Cataloging in Publication Data

Short, Luke, 1908–1975.
  The man from two rivers / Luke Short.
    p.   cm.
  ISBN 0-7838-1466-6 (lg. print : sc)
  1. Large type books. I. Title.
  [PS3513.L68158M35 1996]
  813'.54—dc20   95-32169

The Man
from Two Rivers

1

The lone man in the skiff shipped his oars and stood up, bracing his shins against the thwart to keep his balance. He looked upriver and saw that the sheeting rain bearing down on him was only minutes away.

His skiff was much closer to the south bank of the wide Seville than the north bank and it was the near bank, with its tall moss-draped trees rising out of a huge green-slimed swamp, that he studied.

The current drifted him to and almost past an inlet to the swamp when he saw it through the break.

There, her lower deck almost awash, was the wreck of a small sternwheeler. It vanished from his sight as the current moved him downriver.

That's got to be her. She sank in a swamp, they said.

Hobe Carew put his oars in the water, turned the skiff around and began pulling up, looking over the shoulder of his duck jacket for the opening of the inlet. He was a tall, wide-shouldered man dressed in worn range clothes and cowman's boots. His dust-colored

Stetson hid thick black hair and shaded his eyes, which were as dark as any Indian's.

As he pulled in to the inlet the first big drops of rain began to dimple the water.

The slime and weeds of the swamp tugged at his oars, almost pulling them from him, and he leaned heavily on his oars to keep momentum.

Just as he finished a stroke and paused to let the weeds trail off, a gun went off behind him. Its crash was simultaneous with the gush of water that erupted alongside the skiff. He could hear the bullet whining off in a ricochet.

Turning on the seat, he noted that he was quartering on the wreck. On her lower deck, he saw through the increasing rain, a woman was levering a fresh shell into the carbine in her hands.

"Quit it! Quit it! I only want out of the rain!" he yelled.

"Go back!" the woman called shrilly.

There was a quality of uncertainty in her voice that Hobe thought he read rightly. He turned his back on her and began to move the stalled skiff through the weeds toward the wrecked sternwheeler, his back crawling. If she really meant to shoot him she couldn't miss at this decreasing distance, even sighting through the now driving rain.

When he felt and heard the skiff bump the wrecked hulk he shipped his oars and, turning

8

away from where he reckoned the woman to be, he scrambled for the bow seat, picked up the painter and climbed gingerly to the deck, then looped the painter over a deck cleat.

Afterwards, he rose from all fours and moved out of the rain to the shelter of the Texas deck, wiped his face with his jacket sleeve and only then looked about him.

The woman — no, the girl — was also standing in the shelter under the Texas deck, her carbine held waist high and pointed at him.

"Take that damn thing off cock," Hobe growled. "It might go off."

"It stays where it is," the girl said quietly. "What do you want?"

Hobe didn't answer immediately, only studied the girl with open curiosity. She could have been eighteen, but not much older. She wore men's clothes. The trouser legs were rolled up over and over; the leather jacket almost reached her knees; her collarless blue shirt was held together at the neck by a piece of string, but the shoes were her own. She was a medium short girl in a big man's clothes, with her chestnut hair braided in two pigtails that hung over each shoulder. Her gray eyes held both fear and anger, but her chin was firm and her wide mouth determined, her nose small and faintly uptilted.

"How'd you get here?" Hobe asked. "Why are you here?"

9

"I ask the questions, you answer them. What do you want here?"

"To get out of the rain."

"There's plenty of big trees out there you could get under."

"All dripping," Hobe said. In spite of the shelter he was cold and his teeth were chattering. "You got a fire in there?"

"No."

"You're lying . . . I smelled smoke."

"All right, I'm lying. But you're not going inside."

"Not going into my company's packet? You're not only trespassing, sis, but you're crazy."

He didn't wait for the rifle barrel to sag; he turned his back to her, then headed for the double door that opened on the lounge.

It was a large room, once carpeted, but the carpet had been stripped and taken. A huge barrel stove, too heavy to transport, was centered in the room and glowing hot, a pile of splintered boards beside it. A big rectangular table was in front of it — the dining area — but the dozen chairs that must have belonged with it were not there. Whatever chairs, sofas, tables and lamps that had furnished the lounge had been taken.

He moved over to one of the cabins, four to a side, that opened onto the lounge. A neatly made up bedroll was on the floor. Nothing else, except a dress hanging in the uncurtained closet, remained in the cabin. The sternwheeler had been looted, stripped of everything that could conceivably be loaded into a small boat.

As he came out of the cabin he saw the girl enter the lounge through the door he had come through. She came over to the stove, her rifle dangling from her right hand, and he moved over to join her. She moved away from him, keeping her safe distance, when he halted and put his back to the welcome warmth of the stove.

She brushed a braid off her shoulder and said, "I'm sorry I was so unfriendly, but I'm alone here. My name is Stacey Wheeliss."

"Mine's Hobe Carew. Like I asked out there, what are you doing here?"

"I came with my father."

"Then those clothes you're wearing are his. He on board?"

"No." She took a deep breath, sighed, and said, "He's dead."

The only thing Hobe could think of to say was, "I'm sorry for that." Then he asked, "When did he die?"

"Two days ago," the girl said.

Hobe was silent for a moment, then said, "That's why you didn't want me here. Is his body aboard?"

"No. Yesterday I put the body in the boat, got out to the river and — and shoved him overboard. I couldn't find any tools to dig a grave with." Her tone was listless, wholly

11

uncaring and indifferent; oddly, it angered him.

He said coldly, "You made the river. Why didn't you drift down until you came across a camp or a cabin where there were people who'd bury him?"

"I couldn't. I'm wanted by the law. So was he."

Hobe silently watched her. Every time she opened her mouth, she shocked him anew. Had she killed her father, he wondered. He said, "Stacey, start from the beginning."

"Some beginning," she said dryly. "I never saw my father until a week ago. I can't remember my mother. She gave me to a friend of hers and lit out."

"This friend raised you?"

"She and her husband. She runs a boarding house. As soon as I could make a bed and carry a platter of steaks, they yanked me out of school and put me to work. No pay, only clothes and food and a bed in the attic."

"So you feel pretty sour about what's past."

"You're damn right I do!" she erupted. She didn't speak for moments, and then said with no sign of temper, "I'm young, but I've never been young. I've been old since I was eight. I've — oh, forget it!"

"Why's the law looking for you and your father?"

Stacey shrugged. "I only know what my father picked up in the river towns. I'd hide in

12

the brush. He'd go in town and listen. Then we'd travel at night. We're wanted because we're supposed to have stolen money from the boarding house."

"But you didn't?"

"No. It's a lie! They want me back there! Once I'm back I'll be broke again. Dad knew it! I think that's what brought on the stroke he died of!"

Hobe rubbed his jaw, scowling. "What'll you do? You can't live here forever."

"Almost. The kitchen is full of preserved stuff nobody bothered to take. I'll wait until they've forgotten me, drift downriver and change my name." She paused, then added, "You know anybody down there that would give me work?"

"No," Hobe said gruffly. Then, "I lied to you, Stacey. I don't work for the people that owned this boat. I'm on the run, just like you are."

Stacey started to lift the rifle, thought better of it and let it settle back. "What did you do?"

"Caught a crew cutting my fence. I shot a couple of them. Trouble was the whole bunch was working for Lew Seely. He's a county commissioner that owns half the grass in the state and wants the other half."

Stacey was watching him and suddenly started to laugh. Puzzled, Hobe waited until she was through. Before he could ask what was funny she said, "I'm asking just what you asked me a minute ago. 'What'll you do? You

13

can't live here forever.' "

Hobe laughed softly in appreciation. Here they were, two strays on the dodge, wanted for crimes that were never committed, or in his case, were justified. He began to pace the big room, his boot heels making a racket he was not aware of at the moment. He slowly circled the stove and Stacey, then stopped, facing her.

"How'd you know about this wrecked boat?" he asked.

"Why, Dad came up on a river steamer. The captain pointed it out, and he remembered." She frowned, then asked, "How did you?"

"Everyone along the river knows it. They helped loot it." Abruptly he changed the subject. "You own a ring?"

"Now I do. I took off Dad's wedding ring. Why on earth did you ask that?"

"You and me are going to be husband and wife — pretend to be, that is. First, we go back to your town and make them drop the charges against you. As your new husband I can raise total hell. Then we'll go back to where I shot the water stealer. I'll get that squared away, too."

"Fine, except what do we use for money?"

"I've got some. Enough to rent a house. You know how to run a boarding house. Well, run it. I'll have a job, I always have had."

Stacey was silent for a full minute, eyeing him with open curiosity. Then she said, "I'll run a boarding house anywhere but here. And when we go upriver we won't be married." At Hobe's nod of agreement she said, "What's got into you? So quick and certain."

"I don't like running, never did, never will. You don't like it either. Together, we won't have to."

2

"I've seen you around town since you was a kid," Marshal Hood said to Stacey. "I hated to put out a pick-up on you."

"Then why did you?" Hobe asked gently.

The three — Stacey in a dark blue dress — were seated in the clean but tiny office abutting the four-cell jail of Riverbend, where they had arrived by steamer late the day before. The marshal, whose name was Ben Hood, was a tall and thin white-haired man in his sixties whose big wide hands bespoke years behind a plow. His bib overalls, straw hat on the desk and his Congress gaiters bore this out. With his square and office-pale face, Hobe thought him to be the unlikeliest lawman he'd ever seen.

"Why the pick-up? Why, both the Comptons come in and claimed their money was gone. So was Wheeliss and Stacey here," the marshal explained.

"How did you know there was any money? Did you see it?"

"How could I? It was gone. I saw where they hid it, though."

Hobe looked at Stacey. "Did you know where they hid it?"

"No," Stacey said, nodding her head in negation. "They were hiding it from me and the roomers."

Hobe looked at the marshal. "You search the place, marshal?"

"For what?"

"The missing money. For all any of us know it could be in a bottom drawer somewhere in the house, couldn't it? Or buried in the cellar. Or anywhere."

The marshal reflected on this for a moment, then said reasonably, "Yes. I reckon it could. But I can't look everywhere."

Hobe came to his feet. Unbuckling his shellbelt with holster, he came over and laid them next to the marshal's hat on the desk, asking, "Would Compton be off work by now?"

"Yes. He works on his own, cuttin' wood for the steamers. He come through town about an hour ago. I reckon he's unloaded by now."

"Let's you and me go talk with him."

"What for?"

"I'll tell you on the way over." He looked at Stacey. "Go back to the boarding house, Stacey. I'll be with you in a while."

"She stays right here," the marshal said.

"Not any longer. Not ever. She's not on the run; if she was, why did we come back here?"

"Well, just don't leave town," the marshal said to her.

Stacey rose, saying, "As long as my husband is here, I'm here. Where he goes I go." She left, closing the door behind her.

Marshal Hood only shook his head, then pulled open a lower drawer of his rolltop desk, dumped Hobe's shellbelt in it and closed the drawer. Then he rose, saying, "Compton's place is just up the way and a block over. We can walk it."

Out on the wide street that was flanked by docks, small warehouses and the river on one side and paint-starved false-front business buildings on the other side, they turned up the street. Except for a dozen or so big cottonwoods that had been preserved for shade, it was a drab river town, smelling of smoke from early supper fires, dust from the freight teams, and always the river's mud. They walked in the road, for there were precious few feet of boardwalk and shade.

"What was you going to tell me in there?" the marshal asked.

"Only that you've been suckered by the Comptons. They wanted Stacey back at work for them and you sure as hell obliged with your pick-up warrant."

"You don't know that!" the marshal said,

close to anger. "Why is she so damn valuable to them?"

"Because she worked free for them for ten years. They fed her, bedded her and bought her a new dress when she wore out the old one. No cash money was ever paid her." He looked at Hood to see if this was registering. It was, but barely. He added then, "Hell, the slaves in Alabama had it better. No, maybe just the same, and that's what we fought a war about. And you, by the Lord Harry, issued the fugitive-slave warrant, like a good, southern sheriff."

Hood was silent for long moments, then asked, "You goin' to make trouble at the Comptons'?"

"All I can," Hobe said. "That's why I asked you to come along."

They were silent as they headed for the Comptons'.

The Comptons' house, with its "Room and Board" sign nailed on the railing of its small front porch, had started out as a big log cabin. Frame additions had been built on either side of it and over it. Except for the grudging porch, no effort had been wasted in trying to make it attractive. It was a big two-story shoebox, a kennel for transients and the uncaring. This nothing, Hobe thought, was where Stacey had spent her remembered life, and he was quietly angry, with whom he didn't know.

A racket of hammering came from behind the house and Marshal Hood said, "That's Les workin' out back. Let's go around."

The narrow front and side yards were uncared for and abandoned to weeds. The back yard was one huge vegetable garden that showed care and attention. Beyond it lay a mounded vegetable cellar and past it a small stable and wagon shed flanked by a tiny corral holding four big horses. It was by the latter a big and brawny man was working on a wheel of a huge, high-sided wagon. He had a rear wheel off and was greasing the axle. At the sound of their footsteps he turned his head and scowled at them. When he recognized the marshal a grin of welcome lit his dark and surly face; he put the paddle back in the bucket of axle grease and rose, wiping his hands on his filthy denim pants. He was tall and well muscled, as any woodcutter or tie-hacker had to be.

Hood spoke first. "Hi, Les." He gestured to Hobe. "This here is Hobe Carew. He wants to talk to you, he says."

Compton's muddy brown eyes were instantly suspicious. His long, unshaved horse face settled into what Hobe guessed was its normal sullen cast. "What about?" he asked curtly.

"Stacey Carew."

"I know Stacey Wheeliss. Don't know a Stacey Carew."

"My wife," Hobe said. "She's here in town. I brought her back."

Compton covered his surprise quickly. "To go to jail? You're some husband."

"She won't go to jail, but I think you might."

Compton took a slow step forward, his big hands unconsciously fisting. He looked at the marshal's bland face and then at Hobe. "Why do you reckon I'd go to jail?"

"For lying her into a false arrest. Your money was never stolen — if you had any. Show me a bank statement proving you had some money."

"I don't hold with banks, never have!" Compton said angrily.

"You hid it then?"

"I sure did, and Stacey knew where. I showed the marshal where we kept it!"

"If he didn't see any money and you can't prove you had any, then how does he know it was stolen?" Hobe asked dryly.

"He knows us! He trusts us! How come Stacey and her old man left early in the morning and we found the money gone just a little later? If they didn't steal it, who did?"

"You did," Hobe said. "She's left you and you wanted her back. Once she was back you'd drop the charge against her on the condition she'd work for you again."

Hobe heard his dog-growl of anger just before he charged, aiming a roundhouse swing at Hobe's head. Hobe bent his knees to duck

20

it, and drove a savage left into Compton's gut just below the ribcage. Compton's explosion of breath was close to a yell. Compulsively his arms came down to wrap around his belly, and he bent over, gagging for breath. Hobe moved in and chopped down savagely at his exposed neck. Compton fell to his knees, howling with pain.

Hobe didn't hesitate for even a moment. A kick to Compton's jaw swiveled his head and he was falling backwards, his legs unmoving.

As Compton crashed to the dirt, Hobe felt his arms strongly seized from behind. Marshal Hood, close on his back, said, "Quit it! Quit it, will you? He's out. You want to kill him?"

Hobe relaxed, and his arms were freed immediately. "I don't mind. He deserves it."

The marshal passed him and halted, looking down at the unconscious, sprawled form of Compton. Then the marshal's gaze shifted to Hobe. "You're a rough one."

Hobe said nothing, catching his breath.

They were both regarding Compton when they heard the back door slam. Together they looked over the garden and saw a gaunt woman in an apron charge down the steps and run down the cinder walk that bisected the garden.

"You let me handle this," the marshal said quietly. "You've talked enough."

Mrs. Compton reached them, halted, looked

down at her unconscious husband, then at the marshal and finally at Hobe. To him she said shrilly, "I saw you kick him! Who are you anyway?"

"He's Hobe Carew, Stacey's new husband, Leila."

Mrs. Compton was a thin, homely woman in her forties. Her brown hair was parted in the middle with a braided bun covering each ear. She knelt by her husband and, using her apron, wiped the blood from his lips and nose, chin and cheeks. Then she looked up at Hobe with hatred burning in her close-spaced amber eyes.

"You'll pay for this!" she said savagely. She looked at Hood. "I want this man arrested, marshal. Attacking a man on his own property, and you watching it!"

"Easy does it, Leila. He'll come around in a bit. No sense moving him now. You get up, hear?"

Mrs. Compton rose, looking at the marshal with uncertainty.

"You and me are going to talk some. Come over here," the marshal said. He walked over to the wagon shed, Mrs. Compton trailing behind him.

They were out of Hobe's earshot, but he could see them. Marshal Hood was doing the talking. Mrs. Compton would nod affirmation now and then; suddenly she lifted her bloody apron to her face and began to cry and wail.

Marshal Hood left her, his face flushed and angry, and headed back to Hobe, who was still standing at Compton's feet.

The marshal halted by Hobe. Before he spoke he sighed. "Well, you were right all the way, Carew. They hid the money up in the attic, then brought their cock-and-bull story to me. They were going to drop charges, like you said, if she was brought back to work. They figure they raised her and she's theirs."

"Can you get word on the river she's not wanted?"

"Tomorrow upriver. Next day down. Yes, the charges are dropped."

Hobe gestured toward Compton. "Want some help with him?"

"Leave him lay there," the marshal said bitterly. "Leila thinks she's so damned smart, let her figure a way to get him inside."

They headed for the street together and Hobe saw that the marshal was cooling off. He'd been made a total fool of by the Comptons, and it rankled.

Suddenly Marshal Hood, as if in rumination, said, "I remember now." He looked sideways at Hobe. "I got a reward dodger in my office on you."

Hobe nodded. "For murder, I reckon."

"No. Attempted murder."

Hobe hauled up and Hood halted too. "You mean I didn't kill him?"

"It didn't say 'Murder.' It said 'Attempted

Murder.' That sure means you didn't kill him."

Hobe laughed silently, so that Hood asked, "What's funny?"

"I'm going back to Two Rivers. I'll get a second crack at him. What's the reward on the dodger?"

"A hundred dollars. Not much, but enough to keep you out of town. Any bounty hunter could shoot you in the back and claim you resisted a citizen's arrest."

"I'll watch my backtrail."

Marshal Hood did not comment, but he looked vaguely displeased. When they reached the marshal's office, Hood unlocked the door and went over to the desk, took out Hobe's shellbelt and gun and extended them to Hobe. While Hobe was strapping on his shellbelt, Hood said, "I wish I could keep you from taking that. It's going to get you in trouble."

"You can," Hobe said. "All you have to do is claim the reward."

Hood passed his hand across his face in a gesture of disgust. "After what you did for me today? I wouldn't even try. Matter of fact I take back what I said — that I wish you wouldn't pack a gun. Still, you'll be in enemy country and I suppose you have to pack it."

As he finished strapping on his shellbelt and gun, Hobe said laconically, "That's about it." He extended his hand, and the marshal rose and shook it. "Thanks for your help, marshal."

"Same here," Marshal Hood said. "Keep in touch, will you?"

Hobe said he would, then left the office, heading downstreet toward the bank and then the boarding house where Stacey was waiting for his news that they were both free.

3

It was barely daylight when Hobe was roused by the distant hoot of the steamer coming upriver. As he rolled out of his blanketroll beside Stacey's bed he guessed that the steamer had already loaded wood from the downriver cache and would spend precious little time loading and unloading here.

He dressed quickly and then moved over to the bed where Stacey was still asleep. She was beautiful, he thought, and blessedly, she didn't know it.

Shortly after noon of the third day upriver, they coasted into the wharf abutting the big, frame warehouse. For the moment the view of Fort Monroe was hidden from Hobe's sight, but he could name every building that was blocked out and hidden. The fort itself was guarded on three sides by adobe walls which were in reality the rear of connecting buildings that faced the parade ground inside. At its big main gate, which now would be open, was a sentry. At each corner of the rectangle was a guard tower. Inside that rectangle and on the front facing the river were headquarters' offices. On the right and inside were married officers' homes, some frame, some adobe. Facing them across the parade ground were the bachelor officers' quarters adjoining the mess hall. At the far end connected to the mess hall were the barracks. Outside the walls and away from the river were the big stables and adjoining corrals, since this was a cavalry post, and cluttered beyond the stables were big feed barns. Facing the stables were the married enlisted men's adobe quarters, and the laundry and bakery.

A hundred yards downriver, off the military reservation, was a big two-story adobe building that housed the settlers' quarters, a big store and saloon which sold liquor only by the drink, not by the bottle. Part of the second story was a hotel and dining room.

Hobe, blanketroll over his shoulder, headed directly for the log and adobe buildings outside of the fort's walls, on the downriver side. These housed the enlisted men's families. Children were playing games on the grassless ground in front of their homes.

The door of the Byers' neat log cabin was closest and Hobe knocked. In a moment it was opened by a big and tall, almost gray-haired half-breed Cherokee Indian who stepped aside, swung the door wider and said, "Where the hell you been, boy? Get in here."

Hobe stepped inside, giving Jim Byers an affectionate thump on the shoulder as he passed. Jim, his trusted friend, had been chief of Indian Scouts when Hobe had been an Army guide.

Hobe looked around the familiar comfortable room that befitted a house which had sheltered four children, now grown and gone. Multicolored, heavy Indian blankets hid the puncheon floor. The rocks at the mouth of the big fireplace were chipped and smoke-stained. The chairs were homemade, with rush and leather seats. The sofa under the front window was a school bench covered with corduroy over goose down. The only wall decorations were rifles and bows.

"Where'd you run that old skiff of mine?" Jim asked.

Hobe then told him of holing up on the wreck of the *Robert O. Reeve* and of finding Stacey there, on the run too. It was only then, he explained, fed up with running, they returned to Riverbend to get Stacey's charges dropped that he learned he wasn't wanted for murder.

Jim nodded and said, "I wondered when you'd know. Hell, your dead man's walkin' the streets of Two Rivers. Not even a sling for his arm. Saw him four-five days ago." Watching Hobe, he scowled, "You goin' in there mad, Hobe?"

Hobe nodded. "Mad and lonesome. Seely's crew is just too many to fight, but I aim to."

"You could use some help. I mean in ways you don't know yet."

"Tell me," Hobe said quietly, inwardly dreading what was coming.

"I took a look at your place," Jim went on. "All your wire's cut. Your barn's burned flat. They tried to burn the house. They got the roof, but the house logs didn't catch. The tent and all your stuff with it is burned out. Lucky you brought your horses to me. Your corral is wiped out. You start damn near over."

Hobe rose slowly and began pacing the floor, hands in hip pockets, head down. Jim was silent, watching him. Hobe halted abruptly, looking at Jim. "Sheriff Inglish know about this?"

"He knows all right, but ain't botherin' to look. If he had, he'd have seen Lew Seely's stock waterin' right in front of your house."

Hobe nodded. "I think I'm making a call on Burt Inglish tomorrow," Hobe said slowly.

"Not alone, you're not. Right now you're open for any cheap shot anybody throws at you. I'll side you."

Hobe nodded, stopped circling the room and looked at Jim. On his face was a malevolent scowl that Jim read and was silenced by.

"I'll be needing more help, Jim. Who do I look for?"

"Well, you've got me for ramrod," Jim said.

Hobe smiled. "You said it, but I was going to ask you anyway." He sat down beside Jim and said, "I've had a lot of time to think after my pull-out, Jim. I was running from the law, I thought; now, after what you tell me, I was running from Lew Seely." He glanced sideways at Jim. "What happened to my place — has it happened to other places around here?"

"Where you been, boy?" Jim asked.

"Not here," Hobe said sourly. "I filed on my land and left the rest of it pretty much up to you when I was loaned out to Fort Abbott."

"Yes, what happened to your place has happened already lots of times. I tried to tell you that way back, but you wasn't listenin'."

"I am now, but who'd it happen to?"

Patiently Jim gave the names of a dozen men, some single, some married, some with children. "He goes after 'em one at a time. Alone they can't handle the LS crew. Their wire's been cut, their beef drove off and scattered and their places have been burned, like yours."

"What happened to these men?"

"Different things. Some pulled up stakes and got out, some were scared, some sold out for a tenth of what they put into their places, others had their places burned."

"Any of them still around?" Hobe asked.

"Some," Jim conceded. "There's old Parry at the freight office. Had a nice place east of the LS. His boy was dry-gulched one night on his way home from town. The old man couldn't buck it alone and moved out. Couldn't sell the place because nobody would buy it after what happened to his boy. Then there's Bill Senior, he does some surveying. Harry Waters lost his woman and he plain walked away from his place. There's others, if I can remember 'em."

"How do they feel about Lew Seely?"

"Like you do, and like you there's not a hell of a lot they can do about it."

"Would they throw in with us to fight Seely?" Hobe asked.

Jim thought for a moment, looked down at the floor and then scrubbed his face with his open palm. "Damned if I know. So much of it was a long time ago. Nobody's got any younger. They're makin' a livin' now and maybe they like it that way." He looked closely at Hobe. "You got anything in mind?"

"No," Hobe answered. "It's come too fast, but if you've got enough men still mad at Seely, maybe we could think of something."

"It'd have to be better than good," Jim said slowly. "They'll take a look at what they're buckin'. The richest man in the state, I'd guess you'd call him. He's got a tame sheriff in his hip pocket. He's got a crew that could fight it out with a troop of cavalry."

"There's a way around everything. We've got to think about it, Jim."

They were both brooding on the problem when the door opened and a slim, dark-haired woman, a flour-sack apron tied around her waist over her black dress, halted just inside the door. It took her no time at all to recognize Hobe. She ran into his open arms and they hugged each other, each gently patting the other's back. She smelled strongly of lye soap, a good smell and an appropriate one, Hobe thought.

Anna backed away a step, holding Hobe by his upper arms. "You know you didn't kill a man. Jim already told you?"

"I heard about it downriver. That's why I'm back, Anna. Partly why, anyway."

"Tell me why only partly. First, let me get out of this wet dress." She left them and went into their bedroom.

Jim said, "She wears that damn wet dress home even in winter. She's lucky to be alive."

"*You're* lucky she is."

When Anna quickly reappeared, she repeated, "Partly why, you said, Hobe. Why partly?" She sat down in the chair closest to Jim.

"Tell her what we've been talking about, Jim."

Jim said it briefly. He was going to side Hobe as long as he was needed. That meant he would be gone for weeks, maybe months, until they got Hobe's place in the shape he'd left it. There'd likely be some fighting and neither Hobe nor Jim wanted her around when that happened. Therefore she'd stay

31

home until he sent for her.

To this news, Anna only nodded, although she could not hide her disappointment.

When Hobe was sure she wouldn't talk any more about this, he leaned forward, put his elbows on his knees and said, "Maybe I got a better idea than Jim's, Anna. He doesn't know about it, so you both listen."

Hobe went on to tell, in more detail than he had told Jim, about finding Stacey on the wreck of the *Robert O. Reeve*; about the death of her father and of their mutual decision to quit running. Their plans for Stacey's future were definite; on the next steamer she was going to follow him up to Two Rivers, rent a house and open a boarding house. Within her short and almost total lifetime she had acquired the knowledge and experience needed to run a boarding house.

Continuing, Hobe told them that she would have enough money from him to pay two or three months' rent on a house until she could attract customers and tenants. Still, she couldn't cook, shop, make beds and keep accounts and do a dozen other things necessary to running her place without help.

Now Hobe concentrated his attention on Anna. "Instead of washing clothes six days a week and living alone, how would you like to lock up this place and work for Stacey?"

"Work for an eighteen-year-old? It's like workin' for my daughter."

"No, my guess is she'll be working for you, Anna," Hobe said. "She knows everything it takes to run a boarding house, but no eighteen-year-old has grownup judgment. That's where you'd come in."

Hobe looked at Jim. "You wanted Anna to stay here until we're past the trouble. Have you thought she might be safer in town with Stacey than here, Jim? Anna would be alone here once you're hooked up with me. All Lew Seely would have to do would be to send a couple of his hardcases down here and take her. Even if you live on the edge of the Army post, that wouldn't be hard."

Jim was silent for long moments, frowning at his fisted hand, then his glance raised to Anna and he said, "It's your choice, Anna. A town's more protection, isn't it?"

"Yes, I'd rather be there, Jim. If Hobe thinks I can help her manage this, then I'd like to go."

4

They were up well before daylight and working by lantern light. Jim hitched up the team to the spring wagon, while Hobe loaded their gear into it. Knowing that they would eventually wind up at Hobe's HC, they had to start from scratch. Blankets were plentiful, a

33

stove was not needed, food could be bought, and the necessary pots and pans were handy and loaded.

When the wagon was finally loaded it was only a light load. Anna, wearing a buckskin jacket and Stetson against the morning chill, called from the doorway, "I'm lockin' up, Jim. Got everything?"

"Lock it up," Jim called back.

She came over to the wagon and Hobe handed her up and gave her the reins. "When you get to my place just find some shade. Don't do a thing. We might even be there before you are."

"Yell first. I'll be taking a bath."

After Anna had driven off, Hobe and Jim shouldered their saddles and moved over to the huge tangle of corrals by the cavalry stables. At the visitors' corral they saddled up two of Hobe's horses, then, driving the remaining three of his remuda ahead of them, headed out for Two Rivers at a brisk trot into the new day.

Two Rivers — so named because it had been built at the junction of the broad Seville and the smaller Clearwater rivers — was an odd mixture of cowtown and river town. This was the end-of-river traffic, for both rivers boiled out of the high and forbidding Dexter range, whose foothills started immediately west of this county-seat town.

Both rivers were bridged above the town where the rivers were narrower. It gave any rider heading for the town the impression that he had entered it by the back door, for the bulk of the town, its cabins, stores and even the brick courthouse, lay down on the flats to the east of the triangle between the two rivers.

Across and beyond the bridge they pushed their horses down the wide main street. Both men were watchful, especially for oncoming riders. Finally, approaching the courthouse, Jim said, "You drop off at the horse shed at the courthouse, Hobe. I'll leave the horses at the stable corral and be back."

Hobe nodded and just before they reached the courthouse he pulled off the street and headed for the open-faced shed holding a half-dozen of the county employees' ponies.

He watched the slow traffic of single riders and freighters, some of whom he knew. And then Jim came into sight and cut behind the courthouse, heading for the shed.

Jim put up his horse, and together he and Hobe headed for the stone steps leading up to the courthouse. Both men knew the sheriff's office was a big room at the right rear corner of the first floor. On their way there, Hobe pulled out his gun and extended it to Jim, who took it, rammed it in his belt, then said, "Why?"

"You'll see."

The door to the sheriff's office was open and

Hobe led the way inside. Ahead of him and against the opposite wall, facing the door, were two flat-topped desks. One, a large one that was backed by filing cabinets. The chair behind the other was empty, but at the big desk sat a middle-aged man with a star on his buttonless vest. At first sight his face and upper body seemed gaunt to the point of emaciation, but that was deceptive, Hobe knew. Even at this age he was a formidable brawler.

Hearing their footsteps, Sheriff Burt Inglish looked up, his pale gray eyes inquiring. When he recognized them both a smile twisted his thin mouth and he tossed the pen he'd been using on the desk.

"Well, well. Decided to give up, did you, Hobe?"

"I was captured and disarmed by Jim here. He brought me in, so he's claiming the reward money." Hobe looked at Jim, who was regarding him with open surprise.

The sheriff leaned forward, clasping his bony hands together and looked first at Jim, then back to Hobe.

"But you and Jim are friends, aren't you?"

"Nothing on the reward dodger said an enemy of mine had to bring me in, did it?" Hobe asked quietly. "Nothing about the reward being payable on my arrest and conviction. No, it was just an invitation to everybody to shoot me in the back and collect a hundred dollars for it."

"I don't rightly remember how it was worded. Does it matter? You've been brought in and you're under arrest." Sheriff Inglish's voice was toneless, holding both boredom and finality.

"How would you remember? Lew Seely likely wrote it and gave it to the printer. County business, I reckon."

"That's his right," the sheriff said offhandedly.

"So what you aim to do with me?"

"Lock you up and try you for attempted murder," the sheriff said coldly.

"And why did I attempt murder?" Hobe asked.

"Why, you'd fenced off free range that you didn't have a shade of a claim to. They were cutting your wire and you shot at them."

"Tell me about this free range."

The sheriff pulled open the top right-hand drawer of his desk and took a cardboard folder out, opened it and said, "This is taken from the *Two Rivers Sun*, dated March 16, 1883. I'll read it to you. 'Notice. That I, the undersigned, hereby warn and notify the public that the valley branch off Silver Creek, six miles east of Two Rivers and extending from Indian Springs to the north bank of the Clearwater River, is claimed by me as stock range. Signed Hobart Carew.' " He paused and added, "The same notice, same date, was in the *Riverbend Eagle*." He held up the clipping. "You sent this notice into the two papers."

Hobe only nodded assent.

The sheriff continued contemptuously, "They got no legal standing at all. They aren't true legal notices and you know it."

Hobe said nothing and the sheriff continued.

"Your possessory title ain't worth a damn. It's no title at all. You fenced off open range. LS had a right to tear down your wire."

Hobe said mildly, "And burn down my barn and the roof of my house? And flatten my corral and burn my tent?"

"Well, you hurt two of their crew bad," the sheriff said calmly. "They were just gettin' even."

Hobe looked over at Jim, who was watching the sheriff with quiet wrath. Then Hobe moved over to the desk, put both hands flat on its surface and said, "I figured if you talked long enough you'd wind up in trouble. You did, all right."

"What trouble?" the sheriff asked cautiously.

"This. You and Lew Seely and his hardcase crew figured that the wire they tore down was my boundary fence. It wasn't. It was a divider fence. My north boundary is a couple of hundred yards north of that fence." He paused, then asked quietly, "Catching on?"

"Go on."

"Why, the LS crew was trespassing on my homestead and destroying most of it. I had the legal right to defend my property."

The sheriff frowned. "It was a mistake, but not mine."

"It was your mistake four times," Hobe said flatly. "First, you knew what was going to happen and were told to stay away from my place. Second, you didn't know my boundaries. Third, you haven't looked at my place since it happened and fourth, you put a reward on me on hearsay evidence you knew were lies."

The sheriff, his hound's face mottled with anger, looked past Hobe at the far wall, apparently at a loss for words of reasonable denial.

Hobe pushed his advantage. "You said I was under arrest. You still say that?"

Inglish shook his head in negation. "No, now I know the facts."

"Then pay Jim for bringing me in. Do it now."

Not surprisingly, Sheriff Inglish pulled out the top right-hand drawer of his desk, took out a sealed envelope and tossed it on the desk top. It clinked, as five double eagles should. Hobe picked it up and moved over to Jim, extended it, winked and said, "Well done. You only did your duty, so I'll forget it." Solemnly, Jim rammed the money in his hip pocket. All three men knew that the money had been waiting for any bounty hunter who delivered Hobe, alive or dead, no questions asked.

"Now, Sheriff, you, me and Jim are going to ride down Grant Street together. We'll hit every saloon you gave a reward dodger to. You'll collect them."

"Why, I give out a lot of them. I don't know how many."

"Then you'd better remember," Hobe said. "We're going to hit every saloon in Two Rivers. We're going to talk to every owner and every bartender in every saloon with a back-bar mirror and tell the bartender to soap this on the glass, 'Reward on Hobe Carew already claimed.'"

The sheriff scowled. "That's one hell of a job," the sheriff complained. "The word will get around."

"It sure will, and you'll get it around. Now let's go."

5

Stacey caught the first upriver steamer, four days after Hobe had left. She'd spent the intervening days in a painstaking review of everything she would need to open a boarding house.

The most important item on her list was to obtain help in running the boarding house, and she was at a total loss. She knew nobody in Two Rivers and Hobe had volunteered no information as to obtaining a house and help to run it. That would come later, he had told her the night before he left as he gave her a bank draft and instructions to ask the bank for any help she needed. That same night before he left, he gave her the name of a small, family boarding house and its proprietor.

In the late afternoon of the third day on the river, Stacey heard the whistle of the steamer announcing its approach to Two Rivers.

Since she was the only woman aboard, she had been given a cabin by herself. She'd spent most of her waiting hours pacing the deck for exercise and watching the shoreline forests from an armchair she had moved from her cabin under the deck. On those days on the river, she had ample opportunity to anticipate what lay ahead for her, but she stubbornly refused to speculate on the future.

Now a knock on the door drew her to it. It turned out to be a black steward asking if her baggage was ready. He came in and took the medium-size suitcase that held all her worldly possessions. Following him out, she watched the approach to the wharves and warehouses that squatted along the river banks. Beyond she could make out the town and the gathering of people, mostly women, waiting on the wharf. As the steamer drew closer most of them began waving handkerchiefs in greeting.

Since Stacey was on the port side and the starboard was where the gangplank would be lowered from, she made her slow way toward

41

the bow as the line was thrown out to the dockers on the pier. When the ship came abreast of the dock and the gangway was lowered, she let the impatient male passengers go ahead of her, so she was the last passenger off. It was a pleasant sight watching the women greeting their men with hugs and kisses and sometimes only a formal handshake. The passengers and their escorts moved along the wharf toward where their luggage was being manhandled down to the porters. Hack drivers from the two hotels in town were calling out the names of their hotels, while the public hack drivers were chanting, "Anywhere you want to go, folks. Anywhere you want to go."

Stacey went down the gangplank and noticed a woman waiting at the end of it. As she put her foot on the dock, she heard the woman say, "You're Stacey Wheeliss, aren't you?"

Stacey looked at the dark-skinned, middle-aged Indian woman, didn't recognize her and asked curiously, "Do I know you?"

The woman smiled very warmly. "I'm Mrs. Anna Byers. Hobe sent me to meet you. You were the only woman aboard, so you must be Stacey Wheeliss." She put out her hand and Stacey took it.

"You didn't have to meet me, Mrs. Byers, but I'm glad Hobe asked you to."

"He's an old friend. He knew I'd like it." Anna pointed her chin, Indian fashion, toward a group of baggage claimants and said, "Let's go find your suitcase and have the hack driver take it to his hack." As they moved over, Anna said, "Hobe told me after you're settled in to take you to the bank."

"That man thinks of everything," Stacey said lightly.

Anna gave her a sidelong look and smiled. "Sometimes past everything," she said enigmatically.

After identifying her new suitcase, the two women followed the hack driver to his vehicle. While he was stowing the suitcase in the boot, Anna said quietly, "Your room is at Webster's boarding house. You tell him."

Stacey looked at her inquiringly and Anna read the question in her eyes.

She said gently then, "Around here, they don't like takin' orders from an Indian. You'll find out."

When the hack driver returned to the front of the hack he asked Stacey her destination and she told him. Webster's boarding house turned out to be a small frame house on the mountain side of the business district. Just before the hack was pulled up Anna said in a low voice to Stacey, "Tell him to leave your suitcase and you'll sign in later. Let's walk the rest of the way, if you feel like it."

"The rest of the way?" Stacey asked. She was puzzled and faintly resented being handled and directed as if she were a child. Immediately, she was ashamed of herself. Mrs. Byers was only trying to help her, she realized.

The two women climbed down from the hack. Stacey asked the driver to take her suitcase in and tell the Websters she would be back later and that she wanted a room saved for her.

The hack driver asked carefully, "A room for two, miss?"

Anna said, "A room for one."

Before the hack pulled out for its next stop, Anna had started back toward the business district, which they had just passed through. Holding their skirts up out of the dust, they reached the beginning of the boardwalk and the shade of the wooden awnings above it.

Here, Anna stopped and Stacey halted too, facing her. They regarded each other in brief silence, Stacey somewhat bewildered, Anna faintly smiling.

Anna said, "Hobe didn't know it when he left you, but I'm workin' for you, if you want me. My husband, Jim, is workin' for Hobe. We've raised two boys and two girls. They're grown up and gone now, so I know how to cook, wash, make beds and clean and sew. After the stores know who I'm workin' for I can buy for you, too. Whatever pay you name is all right with me."

Stacey smiled. "I want you and need you, Anna. And believe me, there'll be pay. I worked too long without any."

"That's what Hobe said," Anna replied. She looked downstreet. "Let's walk slow to the bank. There's things I've got to tell you."

Side by side they headed down the board-walk at a leisurely pace. Anna did most of the talking. She explained that the bank's owner and president was Lew Seely, who also owned the big LS Ranch. While Hobe was on the run the LS crew had cut his fence, tried to destroy all his buildings and wrecked his place.

Stacey halted, a look of dismay on her face. Anna stopped too.

"I didn't know about this," Stacey said.

"How could you? Hobe didn't know about it either until he got back here." She went on to tell of Hobe's confrontation with Sheriff Inglish and the cancellation and withdrawal of the reward offer for Hobe.

For stunned moments Stacey pondered this wretched news in silence and then they both continued down the boardwalk. Then Anna came to the immediate point. Did Stacey have the bank draft with her? When Stacey said she had, Anna asked her if she had any iden-tification, which would be necessary to vali-date the draft. Hobe had thought of that, Stacey assured her. He had gone to Marshal Hood, who had written a letter of identifica-tion and recommendation to Lew Seely. She had it with her in her handbag.

They were approaching the big, frame two-story building, whose lower floor housed the bank, and Anna halted, as did Stacey.

"I won't go in the bank with you," Anna said. "Nobody in there knows me, but why take chances? Did Hobe tell you what to do?"

At Stacey's nod, Anna said, "They'll question you in there. If you tell them you're lookin' for a place to turn into a boarding house, they'll come up with half a dozen buildings they own paper on. So tell them nothin'. What you do with that money is your business only." She paused. "Worried about anything else?" When Stacey shook her head in negation, Anna said, "I'll be here."

Stacey, alone, headed for the bank. Remembering Anna's last question, she smiled faintly. Was she worried about anything, Anna had asked. Yes, she was worried about everything.

She entered the bank and halted after a few steps inside it. On her right was a long counter with three barred tellers' cages. The first cage was empty, its grill lowered and locked. At the next cage the teller was waiting on a woman whose two small boys were playing a game of tag on the tiled lobby floor. Beyond her and behind the bars of the last cage was an elderly man who was watching the romping children without any amusement whatsoever. His expression indicated the iron disapproval that a church warden might have shown at a game of tag being played between the pews of his church.

Stacey headed for the cage, noting ahead of her the partition of walnut wainscoting and frosted glass which separated the lobby from the rest of the bank. An unmarked door was in its middle.

Stacey moved over to the old man's window, opened her handbag and drew out an envelope, saying, "I have a bank draft here. I'd like to open an account with your bank."

She watched the old man open the unsealed envelope and read the bank draft. He gave her the briefest of looks and then said, "Excuse me, miss. I'll have to check on this. I won't be long."

He turned, took a couple of steps and vanished behind the partition. Stacey could hear a murmured conversation behind the partition. It was brief and ended with the reappearance of the clerk, which was simultaneous with the opening of the door in the partition to her left. Half turning, she saw a tall and lean gray-haired man standing in the door of the partition. He wore a dark business suit, shined black half-boots and a black string tie at the collar of his white linen shirt.

"Miss Wheeliss, won't you come in, please?"

As Stacey headed for the door which was being held open for her by the older man, she suddenly wished for Anna. Immediately afterwards she forgot Anna as Lew Seely closed the door, pulled out an armchair facing his desk and seated her. Circling the desk, Seely never shifted the appraising glance of his green canny eyes from her. Seating himself behind his desk, Seely said, "It's always a pleasure to welcome a new account, Miss Wheeliss." He pushed some papers aside and said while watching her, "I have to ask some questions, Miss Wheeliss, purely routine."

"Of course."

"How old are you?"

"Almost nineteen."

Seely looked at the bank draft on the desk blotter before him. "You have some identification, of course?" he asked.

Stacey reached in her handbag and drew out the letter Hobe had obtained from Marshal Hood. She extended it and Seely leaned forward to accept it.

As he read it, Stacey studied his face. It was a shrewd and guarded face, she thought — handsome and almost unlined, with weather wrinkles at the outer corner of each eye.

When Seely finished reading Marshal Hood's letter of identification he looked abruptly at Stacey. Then he put down the letter, rose and went over to a wooden filing cabinet. After a short search he drew out two pieces of paper, pinned together, closed the file and moved over to Stacey's chair and extended the papers. Stacey took them and Seely returned to his chair as she regarded what he had given her. It was the wanted dodger on her. Attached to it was the letter from Marshal Hood canceling the dodger.

"What happened over there?" Seely asked.

Briefly as she could, and without mentioning Hobe, she told of working for the Comptons and of their making false charges to get her back after she'd left them.

"So you're going to open a boarding house here," Seely said when she'd finished.

Stacey was genuinely surprised. "I am, but how did you know?"

Seely smiled disparagingly. "Most of us work at what we do best. That's what you do best, isn't it?"

When Stacey only nodded, he said, "Well, like all banks, we hold some pretty doubtful paper. We don't push very hard because we'd rather have a house that's being taken care of than an empty one. Still, we're taken advantage of." He rose, and it was unmistakably a gesture of dismissal. "Come around tomorrow and we'll have some places you can look at, if you want."

He circled the desk and opened the door. "You can draw on your money any time. Thank you, and we'll be seeing each other."

Stacey said good-bye and headed for the street door. Was this pleasant and helpful man the ruthless and savage boss of a hard-case crew that Anna and Hobe believed him to be? It didn't seem possible.

She found Anna just where she had left her,

only she was seated on a bench backed up against a storefront. Stacey sat down beside her as Anna asked, "Everything go all right?"

"Not a hitch. He's not the ogre everyone makes him out — at least he wasn't to me. He even offered to check on property the bank has loaned money on."

"Ha!" Anna said. "Did he tell you about tryin' to burn out Hobe? No, you aren't connected, so he wouldn't. Did anybody tell you about burnin' out a big nester family? 'Lightnin,' he said. Does lightnin' smell of coal oil, like that place did? Oh, why go on? What Lew Seely can't scare out of people or cheat out of 'em, he'll burn or wreck. You can't burn land, and that's what he wants — all he can get any way he can get it."

"Well, you know about him, where I don't. Your judgment goes, not mine," Stacey said meekly.

Anna gathered up her handbag and rose. "All you have to do to hate him is listen, just listen. And now, shall we look at the houses I saw?"

6

Well before daylight, Hobe and Jim had their breakfast fire built close to the north wall of Hobe's cabin. They were both dressed warmly against the night's chill off the Dexters.

On their second cup of coffee it happened. The coffee pot on the coals of their open fire erupted with a clang of metal on metal and then came the report of a rifle shot. Both men lunged immediately for their rifles, which were leaning against the wall. Hobe reached his first, and said, "Get inside, Jim. Keep shooting."

Even as Jim was moving toward the back door with his rifle, Hobe, bent low, rifle in hand, was heading for the foothill timber. A second shot tried to find him in the barely beginning daylight, but it wasn't even close. He heard the third shot clunk against the cabin wall and then he eased into the shelter of the piñon.

Hauling up, breathing heavily with the effort of the run, he hid behind the trunk of a big piñon and tried to figure this out. He was immediately certain who had shot at them and why. It had to be one of Lew Seely's crew. It was, he guessed, the beginning of a planned harassment. A hidden sniper could pin them in the cabin for every daylight hour. If they were unable to work outside, it would not be long before they had to abandon the homestead. Hobe was certain that this was Lew Seely's second move to drive him off.

A fourth shot erupted into the coming dawn, but this was from Jim in the cabin. It was answered immediately by a shot from the hill and Hobe made certain of the direction of its

51

source. He knew that Jim's shot was only a decoy to locate the hidden rifle for him.

Hobe, clinging to the screening timber, moved higher into his left as silently as he could. His disadvantage, of course, was that he was afoot while the rifleman, at the first sound of his approach, could mount and ride away with no chance of pursuit.

Again Jim shot and again he drew answering fire from the rifle. Hobe moved uphill, not aiming for the area that hid the rifleman. Again Jim shot and drew a quick two shots from the hill.

When he was fairly certain he was above the rifleman, he halted. This wasn't properly a bushwhack, Hobe knew, for the rifleman, if he could see well enough to hit a coffee pot on the fire, could have seen both of them. It was meant to scare and warn them. His grim hope was that with luck he could change things around.

Softly he cocked his rifle under the sound of the first bird song he heard. False dawn was just graying and he moved stealthily from tree to tree. There was enough light to distinguish the cedars from the piñons and the latter he avoided so as to miss stepping on the dry hulls of last season's piñon drop.

Surely, he thought, the rifleman's horse had to give away his location by the jingle of his bit or of a hoof moving on the rocky ground.

It came, finally, directly ahead of him. A shot from Jim below rocketed through the tree branches, apparently close enough to the horse to bring a quick lip-blubbering exhalation of breath.

Now that he had the horse located, he waited for the rifleman's answer to Jim's last shot. It didn't come. Apparently, with the coming daylight, the rifleman was afraid to locate himself by the flash of his gunfire.

Hobe suddenly heard the sound of displaced rock and gravel that a man might make in walking over broken ground. Swiftly, bending low, Hobe moved silently toward the horse. It gave a whicker of recognition as its owner came closer.

Hobe could see the outline of the horse, and he waited. Presently a man's form moved up opposite the horse and freed its reins from a tree branch.

"I can see you and your horse, *hombre.* First drop your rifle, then your pistol, and damn well throw them down so I can hear them."

He waited, knowing that the man was searching the close timber, trying to locate him, but Hobe guessed he couldn't. "Now," Hobe said flatly.

He heard the heavy clatter of the rifle hitting the rocky ground, then the softer, lighter sound of the six-gun tumbling among the rocks.

"Head downhill. I'll bring your horse."

"I walk down there and I get shot. The hell with you."

"Not if you're afoot. Now move."

With the deepest reluctance, the man turned and headed downhill. He was a bulky man, Hobe could make out in the increasing light, but that was all Hobe could tell about him. He gathered up the reins of the horse and with his rifle at full cock against the chance that his man might make a try for his weapons, he started downhill.

As they neared the edge of the timber, Hobe called, "Come out, Jim. We got company."

Jim was starting a fire as Hobe approached. He dropped the reins and the horse halted immediately. Hobe stepped back and rubbed a hand over the horse's left hip, feeling the old brand burn, which read LS.

Jim's fire was competing with the coming daylight and the LS puncher hauled up by the fire. Hobe circled him and halted by Jim. He took the rifle off cock, leaned it against the cabin and both he and Jim looked at the surly-faced puncher. He was a younger man than Hobe had taken him to be. His meaty face held a sullen defiance as he looked from one to the other.

"Why don't you get his horse headed north, Jim, outside the fence?"

Jim left and the puncher and Hobe watched Jim pick up the reins and lead the horse across the creek. He opened the gate, gave the horse a slap in the rump and then closed the gate behind. Afterwards, Jim headed back for the cabin.

Hobe said to the puncher, "Sit down. Make yourself comfortable. Take your boots off and warm your feet."

"They're warm," the puncher said sourly.

Hobe reached back for his rifle, pointed it and said, "Nowhere near warm enough. Take them off."

"Goddamnit, I'm already afoot! Ain't that enough?"

"No," Hobe said.

Jim came up then and looked quizzically at Hobe.

"Do you take 'em off or do we?" Hobe asked the puncher.

Swearing bitterly, the puncher sat down and worked his feet out of his boots, then rose. His face was red with rage and humiliation. "By God, I'll be back and you'll wish you never seen me."

"I already do," Hobe said. "Now, get off my land."

The puncher started off in the direction of town, bootless, horseless and weaponless. It was full daylight as they watched the puncher's size diminish in the distance.

Jim said then, "If I was him, I'd be back, too."

"So would I," Hobe said. He moved over to the wall, leaned his rifle against it, then squatted on his heels, back against the wall. "You know what this adds up to, Jim?"

"One a day, don't it?"

Hobe nodded. "Every time we move outside the cabin we get chased back inside. Wire cut again. All work stopped. We finally have to quit."

"That's the way it works. He's done it before," Jim said sourly.

"Remember what we talked about at your place? All the men who'd been chased off by Seely?" At Jim's nod, Hobe continued. "You mentioned Parry, the man whose son was murdered. You said he moved off his place but couldn't sell it because everybody was afraid to buy it. What happened to it?"

Jim said dryly, "Just what you'd reckon. Seely moved a crew in. It's the east base camp for LS."

"But Parry still holds title to it?"

"The way I heard it Seely sent him a piddlin' check and papers to sign. Old Parry fired the papers back unsigned. Sent the check back too. I reckon he still holds title. Why?"

"Let's head for town and talk to him. I just maybe got an idea."

Their pull-out took about twenty minutes, for aside from their blanketrolls, some tools and feed, there was nothing to load in the wagon except their saddles and the LS puncher's boots, which they would get rid of on the way to town.

While Jim finished harnessing the team, Hobe took down the rope corral, then moved off close to the creek. Looking across it to the rolling prairie foothills, he wondered if he would ever come back here. Would he, like so many of the men Seely had chosen to destroy, figure it just wasn't worth it against the odds he must face?

Still, he'd faced big odds against him before, and had beaten them. As a matter of fact, he liked them, always had, and he supposed he always would. This land was his. Someday he'd be on it again and he'd stay on it.

In Two Rivers they stored their wagon at the feed stable, saddled their horses and split up, Jim to search for a new boarding house just opened, Hobe to find the Western Freight office and stables, B. Parry, proprietor.

Western Freight was a block off Main Street, close to the docks. It consisted of a big high-roofed wagon shed, a big pole corral holding a dozen sturdy horses. A weathered log cabin facing the street had a modest sign over its front door proclaiming its business.

Dismounting and tying his horse to a corral pole, Hobe started for the office. He guessed the back half of the building was B. Parry's living quarters.

He was almost to the door when it was opened and a burly man stepped out. Seeing Hobe, he didn't bother to shut the door and

Hobe moved through the doorway and was immediately in a cramped office that could barely contain the big rolltop desk, file cabinets and the two worn easy chairs.

Seated in a swivel chair and facing the door was a sparse, gray-haired man wearing an unbuttoned vest over his red-checked calico shirt. His lined, pale face held a gentle melancholy, as did his dark eyes. "Saw you ride in," he said in a mild voice. "What can I do for you?"

"You're Mr. Parry?" At the man's nod, Hobe moved over, extended his hand and introduced himself.

"I just wanted to meet a man who's told Lew Seely to go to hell." They shook hands and Parry gestured to a chair. "A lot of good it did me." He sat down, as did Hobe, and they regarded each other carefully. "Sounds like you got a grudge," Parry said quietly. "What'd he do to you?"

"He's hunting me off my place, same as he did you." At Parry's look of inquiry, Hobe told his story, culminating in the events of the previous night. "I know he'll never let me alone, but I don't aim to let him alone either."

"How'll you manage that?" Parry asked dubiously.

Then Hobe told him Jim Byers' account of what had happened to Parry's son, and his decision to abandon his place. When Hobe told of Jim's account of Parry's refusal to sell his place to Seely, Parry smiled and nodded.

"That's about it," he agreed.

"You still hold title to it?"

Parry nodded understandingly. He swiveled his chair to face the desk and pulled open a bottom drawer. From it he lifted out a cardboard filing case from which he promptly drew out a document. Spreading it on his desk, he said, "That's spelled C-a-r-e-w?" When Hobe said it was, Parry picked up a pen from the inkstand, dipped it in the ink and signed the document. He handed it to Hobe saying, "I assume Hobe is short for Hobart."

"That's right." Hobe read the deed and assignment, then asked, "What's the consideration, Mr. Parry? This is a legal transfer of property."

"A dollar will bind it," Parry said idly.

Hobe rose and found a silver dollar in his pants pocket. Parry accepted it and handed the deed to Hobe.

Hobe said then, "When I'm done, you'll get this back."

Parry shook his head. "Don't want it. There's too much grief tied up in it. Besides, I'm set here."

"Still, you'll get this back." Hobe held out his hand and Parry rose and took it.

"Don't know what you'll find there, even if you get close to it. I left everything except these three chairs and the desk," Parry said. He frowned and then said, "Hanged if I know how to say this polite-like, but I think you're as good as dead. I wish you wouldn't do it, but I can tell your mind's made up. Good luck is all I can say."

"That's all I can say to myself. Thanks, Mr. Parry. You'll be hearing from me or hearing about me."

7

With Parry's signed note in his pocket, Hobe felt he could afford to make some necessary purchases. At a hardware store he bought six wire cutters, some Giant powder, almost endless feet of fuse cord and two cases of .45 caliber ammunition. He paid for his purchases and told the clerk he would pick them up later. He asked the clerk if he knew of a newly opened boarding house in town.

"Passed it yesterday." He gestured, "One block over and two blocks up the hill. A gray frame house with a new sign on it. It'll be on your right. You can't miss it."

Chances were, Hobe thought, there weren't many new boarding houses in a town of this size and this new one had to be Stacey's.

It was about a half-hour before noon when, following the clerk's instructions, he found the sizable gray house and sign, white letters on red hung from the porch eave, advertising, ROOMS AND BOARD. Hobe dismounted and tied his horse to the ring in the stepping block and then regarded Stacey's investment, if it were hers. It was a two-story house with a big many-paned window on either side of the front door. The house needed paint, as did every other building in Two Rivers, but two big cottonwoods flanked either side of the graveled walk. It was a good location, Hobe guessed, and only a short walk from Main Street. He could imagine it attracting a variety of drummers who would like its closeness to business houses and saloons. He went up the graveled walk, mounted the porch steps and twisted the lever of the door bell.

The door was opened almost immediately by Anna, who smiled her welcome. "You didn't have to ring, Hobe. We were expecting you." She stepped aside and Hobe moved into a big room holding three square tables flanked by plain and sturdy chairs. The stairs to the second floor separated this dining room from the kitchen. To his right was a small parlor, holding a leather-covered sofa and occasional chairs.

Anna led the way back into the kitchen, where Stacey was working at the counter below the cabinets. Looking over her shoulder, she smiled at him and dried her hands on her apron. "Anna had this already spotted, Hobe. Isn't it nice?"

Without smiling, Hobe said, "I smell bed-bugs."

"You do not!" Stacey said heatedly. "We went through all the beds."

It was Anna who laughed first and Hobe joined her. When Stacey knew this for a prank, she laughed too, her face flushed with embarrassment.

Of course there was nothing more immediate than for Hobe to see the whole house, since he had made it possible. He was shown the four plain but large rooms upstairs. They were as clean and tidy as two clean and tidy women could make them. Hobe spoke his approval. The two small bedrooms opening off the parlor were shared by Anna and Stacey.

Afterwards they moved into the kitchen and sat at the round table while Anna poured coffee for them. They were both full of women's news. Stacey had established credit at two stores, one a meat market. Both delivered their wares, so that problem was solved.

As Stacey began to stir her coffee Anna took down a straw hat from a wall nail. She said, "None for me, Stacey. I'm goin' to the store for more pins."

When she was gone Stacey put the coffee cups on the table and sat down next to Hobe. "You know, Hobe, Anna is without a doubt the nicest woman alive."

"I've known that for a long time."

"Tell me about her. Not about her house and children, but about her."

"Well, around 1830 the government moved all the Indians to the west of the Mississippi River. Her people were moved into the Cherokee Nation."

"But she's got an education. I should know, because I don't have."

Hobe smiled. "Did she tell you how she got it?" When Stacey shook her head, Hobe went on, "Well, even before the Cherokees were moved out of the South, they were friendly with whites, even then. Anna had three older brothers. She tell you about them?"

"Only that she had them."

"Well, the Catholic fathers started a boys' academy on the new Cherokee land. Her three brothers went to it. When they'd bring their books home at night she'd study along with them. She finally wound up teaching them."

They heard the front door click shut and they both looked, expecting Anna. Instead Jim moved into the room, a faint smile on his face. "Got two that'll throw in with us, Hobe. By tonight we ought to have more."

That night, after supper, two big, square dining tables were shoved together to make one, chairs were moved up, and the six men sat down in no special order. Anna came from the kitchen with an armful of saucers, which she distributed as ashtrays.

Hobe looked around and his glance settled

on Bill Senior as the men fell silent.

"I know Jim asked you this or you wouldn't be here. Still, I'll ask it again. Is there any way Lew Seely can hurt you more than he already has? Do you owe his bank money? Can the commissioners hurt you in any way, because they'll try?"

"I'm married to a commissioner's daughter, but she don't like him any better than I do. And the bank don't have any paper on my saloon or my survey equipment," Bill Senior said. He looked at Andy Chisholm who, in spite of his lack of height and weight, was a young and feisty dock worker.

"No way he can hurt me except kill me, and that takes some doin'," Andy said.

"Same here," Marv Freeman said. "Him or any LS hand shows up, my store is closed. I don't even want their money, but I'd sure like to shoot at some."

"All right, you want to take the fight to him, like I do. Jim here can tell you about Parry's place since they changed it. He stops by every once in a while."

Jim nodded. "Well, they threw up a new 'dobe cookshack-bunkhouse. There's a ton of grub in the storeroom, so we'll eat. I'm good friends with the fat cook, so we don't chase him off. There's a big barn with horse feed. That's where we keep our horses — inside the barn, and guarded. The first thing they'll do is try to get us afoot."

"That'll bring Inglish down on us for damn sure for stealin' feed," Andy Chisholm objected.

"Let him come," Hobe said. "I got title to the place from Parry this morning. Seely don't own it. I do."

"But it's Seely's grub and feed we're usin'," Frank Eastlake said.

"Parry left grub and feed that Seely used. Even trade, I'm saying."

"We're talking like we already have the place. How do we get it?" Freeman asked. He rubbed a half-mashed nose, courtesy of an LS crew.

Hobe looked at Jim, who said, "Go in pairs in the middle of the mornin', half an hour apart, say. Nobody'll be there unless he's down sick. Me and Hobe'll go first. If there's any trouble, one of us will let you know. There won't be, though."

"Then what?" Freeman asked. "Sounds like we're the Army all forted up and they're the Indians." He looked at Jim. "Bad joke, Jim, but you know what I mean."

"I should. I've fought more of 'em than anybody here, except Hobe."

Hobe leaned back. "Well, it's settled then. Nobody's expected at home or his work until he shows up. That's it, isn't it?" When the four men nodded, Hobe said, "We ought to have a remuda of a dozen ponies. I'm short our four because we didn't have time to hunt 'em. I'll fill in from the feed stables. How about the rest of you?"

Each man named the number of horses he could muster. Counting the horses Hobe would get from the stable, the number came to fourteen.

"No reason why each of us can't drive his own string. The whole bunch together might get somebody curious."

He explained then that he and Jim would head south with a team and extra horses right after breakfast. It turned out that Hobe was the only one in the group who didn't know where Parry's place was. First thing they would do would be to turn loose all the LS horses. They could expect that the LS crew, when they found their base camp occupied, would head straight for LS headquarters. The action would start, he thought, the day after tomorrow. Only after they had proved they could defend and hold Parry's place could they travel the LS range. If they could savage the headquarters ranch, part of the LS crew would be penned down to protect it.

After that it was a wrecking mission, Hobe said. Each man in the group had had his land taken by force by LS. Bill Senior's limp came from a rifle slug in his hip. After he was down and disarmed, he'd watched his small spread burned to the ground. Andy Chisholm had been surprised by a half-dozen of the LS crew, beaten senseless and regained consciousness only to watch the biggest bonfire he'd ever seen — his place. Frank Eastlake had been arrested for trespassing on LS range. When he got out of jail he'd found his place taken over by LS; they'd chased him off and seen that he stayed off. Marv Freeman was a Jew who'd had the nerve to buy a small place and run cattle instead of running a junk yard in town. He was beaten until he was almost dead for presuming to own land that should belong only to Gentiles. LS took it over.

When there were no more questions to be asked or answered, Anna and Stacey brought in coffee. Afterwards the meeting broke up, for the following day would be a long one.

Later Hobe and Jim set the dining room straight while Anna and Stacey rinsed out the coffee cups. Finished, the four of them sat at the kitchen table.

"How much did you hear?" Jim asked Anna.

"We're women, you goose," Anna said mockingly. "All of it. We opened the transom a few inches."

Stacey asked then, "Jim, how big a crew does Seely have?"

Jim frowned. "Don't really know, Stacey. He's got a half-dozen line camps. Twenty-five men, maybe more."

"Six against twenty-five," Stacey said slowly. "Four times as many as we have."

"Not as bad as it sounds," Jim countered. "They're scattered over half a dozen counties.

In good weather the men turn the line shacks over to the lice, and camp out. It'd take two weeks to find 'em, round 'em up and bring 'em in."

"But even if he could find half of them, that's twice as many men as we have," Stacey said.

Jim looked at Hobe and smiled faintly. "I don't mind them odds, do you, Hobe?"

"Oh, I mind 'em, but I don't know what we can do about it."

8

It was close to ten o'clock the following morning when Hobe, driving the team, and Jim, mounted and leading the spare horse, came in sight of the LS east base camp. At this far-off look it seemed a barren spot, with no sizable trees even close to it. This pleased Hobe, for anyone approaching in daylight was out in the open. In a night fire fight the only shelter would be the three main buildings — Parry's original log house, the big barn and the new adobe bunkhouse-cookshack.

It was for the latter that Jim headed in the bright June sunlight. Hobe pulled up the wagon in the open doorway of the barn and idly pretended to fuss with the harness, watching the kitchen doorway of the cook-shack. Presently, Jim walked through the doorway and beckoned to him. That meant the crew was out.

Hobe climbed back in the wagon and by the time he reached the building, a dumpy, bald man came out and stood beside Jim. Hobe reined up beside them and Jim said, "This here is Bates Jordan I told you about. He says he's surrendered, so don't shoot."

Bates grinned an almost toothless smile and Hobe reached down to shake his hand.

"This is the damndest," Bates said. "You really mean it, huh?"

Hobe nodded, "Workin' for us, Bates?"

"Hell, if I went back to headquarters I'd only get fired. Sure I am, as long as you can hold the place."

"You're hired. Now, let's unload the stuff in the bunkhouse."

The three of them unloaded the powder and cases of ammunition and stored them in a corner of the bunkhouse. Afterwards, they stripped the big room of all the gear and clothes belonging to the LS crew, pitched them in the wagon, drove out south of the place and dumped them. It took three trips and left a mound six feet high.

By the time they got back to the bunkhouse, the second pair, Senior and Chisholm, were already busy. They had emptied the high-pole corral next to the barn of LS horses and turned their string into it. Hobe drove the wagon into the barn, turned one horse into the corral, saddled the other and then he and Jim rode out to the horse pasture, opened a far gate and hazed the twenty loose horses out into the open range.

"We're goin to see some mad cowboys tonight. A ten-mile ride on tired ponies and no supper," Jim said.

It happened before that. Freeman and Eastlake had just pulled in, Hobe and Jim helping to push their string into the big, high corral, when they all heard a shrill whistle from the direction of the bunkhouse. They looked in that direction and saw Bates Jordan frantically gesturing toward the south.

Hobe was the first to spot what Bates was signaling. Two riders had pulled up their horses by the mound of LS gear; one was dismounted and picking through the pile of clothes and blankets; the other, still mounted, was watching the buildings and activity around them.

Turning his horse, Hobe headed for the two men in the distance, and he heard Jim's horse pull up beside him. As they approached, the two LS riders exchanged words; they were understandably puzzled by what they found.

As Hobe and Jim reined in the mounted rider, a leathery, thin man about fifty, looked from Hobe to Jim, then back to Hobe. "What the hell's goin' on here? That's our stuff. Who are you?"

"Name's Carew. I'm the new owner."

"Wait a minute," the dismounted man said in angry arrogance. He was much younger than the other man, and cocky. "If Seely's sold the place, he'd have told us."

Jim said, "It wasn't his to sell, as you damn well know. Can you read?"

"Good as you, you goddamn Injun!"

Without taking his glance off the man, Jim said, "Show him, Hobe. And be careful with it, you goddamn white man. Anything happen to it and you're dead, right where you're standin'."

Hobe moved his horse over, took the deed out of his shirt pocket and handed it to the truculent puncher, who accepted it, unfolded it and laboriously read it. Finished, he handed it back, saying scornfully, "Hell, that ain't signed by Seely. It ain't worth a damn."

"Just tell your boss you saw it. He'll understand."

The older man had been looking around. He asked, "Where's the horses?"

"We turned 'em loose. They were on my range," Hobe said. "So are you, so get off."

The younger puncher gestured to the pile of gear. "With all this?"

"Come back and get it. Or leave it. The stuff will burn. Just don't come any closer than this," Hobe said.

The two punchers looked at each other, but it was the younger who spoke. "Well, we just might bring some help to haul it away."

"We're counting on it," Hobe said dryly.

The young puncher mounted, but the older man was looking at Hobe. "How many in your crew?"

"There's an easy way to find out," Hobe said. "Now, move."

9

Supper at the big house had been served and Lew Seely left the big dining room for his office in the right wing of the big two-story U-shaped stone building. The sun was low and hidden behind the Dexters, but Perez, husband of his cook-housekeeper, Florita, had lighted the lamps in his corner office.

This was Lew Seely's work place, a spacious room holding a huge rolltop desk against the inner wall, two long leather-covered sofas facing each other on the side walls and a leather-covered easy chair at the far end of each sofa.

Seely had spent the day, one of his two days a week in Two Rivers, at the bank and tonight he intended to review the books already on his desk. Peeling off his coat and unbuttoning his vest, he tossed his coat on the nearest sofa, sat down at his desk and took a cigar from the desk humidor. He was lighting his cigar when a discreet knock sounded on the door at the far end of the room. He was used to that knock, since it came from Dana Keyhoe, the headquarters foreman. Dana never interrupted his lonely meals, but concealed himself close to one of the big cottonwoods outside, waiting until he could see Seely, through one of the side windows, enter his office and only then paid his visit.

Seely swiveled his chair to face the door and called, "Come in, Dana."

The door swung inward and a tall, rangy, middle-aged man dressed in clean range clothes stepped inside the room. As always, he did not take off his hat, which in his view was an act of subservience. He walked over to the desk and halted before Seely.

"What's it this time, Dana?"

"Con Jeffries and a couple of his boys are outside. Have some news for you."

Seely sighed and nodded. "Bring 'em in."

Dana affected an oversized gray moustache whose minutest movement Seely had learned to read as a signal flag. Its motion now settled into a grim line. "You won't like it," Dana said.

"Can't you tell me?" Seely asked.

"I could, but I reckon they'd better."

Seely sighed again. "All right. Get 'em in here."

Dana went to the door, swung it open and called out into the dusk, "Come in, boys."

Led by Con Jeffries, the east camp foreman, two hands trailed him in. Con moved straight for Seely, who stood and extended his hand. When the casual amenities were exchanged, Con turned and said, "You remember Dad Peters, the other one you ain't seen much of, name's Stew Finnegan."

If Dana thought this visit indicated trouble, Seely wanted to charm this pair into being at ease. He moved out past Con and shook hands as both men removed their hats.

Seely said, "Dad, you're looking pretty spry," and then he added, "Sit down, all of you."

Con, a dark-complexioned, undersized man whose square face held a look of anointed authority, seated himself on the sofa closest to Seely's chair, taking off his hat as he sat down. Dad and Stew seated themselves on the same sofa. On the opposite sofa, Dana seated himself close to Seely.

When they were all comfortable, Seely said to the three of them, "Dana says I ought to hear you first. What's this all about?"

Con said, "We got our camp taken over to-day, Lew." He tilted his head toward the other two. "They was there when it happened. You tell it, Dad."

The old man described their noon approach to the line camp and finding the pile of clothes and gear that had been removed from the bunk-house. While he and Stew were looking over the stuff, two men rode from the bunkhouse to meet them, one of them an Indian. The white man claimed he bought the place from

Parry and was taking possession.

Seely came alert then. "What was his name?"

"I don't know," Dad said. "He showed Stew the paper." Dad looked at Stew. "You tell him."

"His name was Carew. Hobart Carew. The deed was signed by B. Parry."

Carew, Seely thought. *Wasn't that the name of the jackleg Army guide that homesteaded north on Silver Creek, the one who put Borden afoot yesterday?*

Stew continued, "I never seen your name on the deed, so I figured he was bluffing."

Seely only said, "Then what?"

"He said we could haul the stuff away or he'd burn it. He said not to come closer than where we were and to get off."

"Got any idea the size of his crew?"

Dad answered, "We only seen two others. They'd chased the remuda out of the horse pasture."

Seely looked at Con. "Then what happened, Con?"

"Same thing," Con answered grimly. "Me and Burkey and Jess stopped to have a look at the pile of gear. Him and this Injun rode up, rifles across their saddles. I told him we hadn't et since before daylight. I said we were tuckered and so was our horses. He said that was just too damn bad, but to get off his land. He gave an arm signal and a couple of shots came from the bunkhouse over our heads, so we left. The rest of the crew has been stragglin' in. They all had the same story."

"They all accounted for?" Seely asked.

Con nodded. "Accounted for and mad."

Seely put his elbows on the chair arm, put palms together, steepled his fingers and looked at the ceiling. Afterwards, he looked at Con and said coldly, "Well, Con, we never signed a contract on this, nobody does. Still, you're boss of the east line camp and its property. You've let the buildings be stolen and the remuda scattered. Everything was your responsibility, but now you come running to me."

"I ain't runnin' to you for help," Con said brusquely. "We need grub and horses. I'll take care of the rest of it myself."

"Do that," Seely said coldly. "You've got the men. Take the place back."

Keyhoe had been listening to this with what seemed the purest boredom; however, he knew it was time to cut it off, because everything had been said. He came to his feet and said, "Mr. Seely's got some night work ahead of him now. Want to say anything more?"

Con stood up and said, "Night, Mr. Seely," put on his hat and headed for the door. Dad and Stew trailed him out, Stew closing the door behind him.

Then Keyhoe said quietly, "Inglish, maybe?"

"Not yet," Seely said.

"A call on Mr. B. Parry."

"It's his to transfer," Seely said wryly.

"Want me to go along with Con tomorrow?"

"That's just what I don't want," Seely said. "Let's see if he's a big boy now."

10

After an early breakfast and chores were done, Hobe sent Jim as a lone lookout and called the rest of the crew together in the bunkhouse, Bates Jordan included. He began by telling them that since there had been no night attack on the place, it was reasonable to assume that an LS crew would appear sometime after midmorning. Then he assigned four men to hole up in and guard the bunkhouse, two at the east windows and two at the west windows. He himself would take an east window. Two men, one of them Bates, who saw no reason for not fighting the men of the boss he despised, and Jim were assigned to protect the barn and the horses in the high-pole corral. All directions were covered and the two in the barn with the hay-loading doors open could protect not only the horses, but the small main house.

"No warning shots?" Andy Chisholm asked.

"Yes," Hobe answered. "First man to sight a rider, give me a yell."

"What if it don't work?" Andy persisted.

"Then we'll be shooting for keeps," Hobe said

flatly. "You think *they* won't be?" He looked at each sober-faced man. "Whatever happens, we can't let 'em push us outside. If they get in, shoot it out in here."

"What if they wait till night?" Freeman asked. "It's too open for a daylight rush."

Hobe grinned. "One thing at a time, Marv."

But Marv was right, Hobe thought. A night attack would be tougher to fight off, but he was counting on the usual total arrogance of LS. To not retaliate immediately would mean a loss of face, an invitation to other dispossessed homesteaders to band together and try what he was trying.

"My guess is that they'll drive a wagon up to that pile of gear to pick it up. That'll attract our attention. When they come at us, it'll be from any direction but that," Hobe said. He looked around at Jim, who had halted in the doorway.

"I wired the corral gate shut," Jim said. "A couple of 'em are bound to come up or down the crick. Those alders will hide 'em until they cut for the corral."

Hobe nodded and stood up. "I reckon you better stay inside for a while. They don't know how many we are and they may have a spotter out there with glasses."

Jim said then, "Bates, you still want in on this?"

"Look, if I'd asked you to keep out a horse for me to ride out on, you'd have given it to

78

me. But I didn't ask, did I?"

Jim laughed. "Come on. Let's you and me head for the barn."

Bates rose as Hobe said, "Get plenty of shells handy to you. All of you. There'll be a lot of flyin' glass too, but I don't know what we can do about that. Now, let's open the windows."

They did just that, then spent an hour smoking, talking about nothing, all of them at their assigned windows when Frank Eastlake called from the south window bay, "Team comin' from the southwest."

Hobe came over and looked out Frank's window. A lone man was seated atop the high-sided wagon; a horseman rode beside the clumsy vehicle.

"You goin' out to meet 'em?" Frank asked.

"No. It gets me out in the open, and that's what they want." He turned and called back into the room, "Look sharp now, boys. This could be it." He went back to his window and took up his vigil.

A long silent two minutes passed before Frank turned and called to Hobe, "The rider stopped, but the wagon's comin' on."

Hobe went over to Frank's window and said, "Let's trade places, Frank."

Hobe replaced Frank at the south window and watched the slow approach of the team and high-sided wagon. There was something more than a little strange about this. One man had stopped at the pile of gear, as ordered yesterday, yet the team and wagon were headed for the bunkhouse. As he watched, the driver of the team picked up a white cloth from the wagon seat and lazily waved it over his head. The wagon was soon within easy rifle range.

Then Hobe had a sudden and overwhelming hunch and he acted on it immediately. Raising his rifle, he took aim at the wagon, not at the driver, but at the wagon box itself. Starting at a spot under the wagon seat, he emptied his magazine, raking the whole length of the wagon about a foot above the bed.

The driver reined in and looked over his shoulder at the wagon bed.

"Here," Frank said from behind him. He extended his own rifle to Hobe and accepted Hobe's, all in the same motion. Again Hobe took aim, a few inches higher this time, and again raked the side of the wagon box. He had fired four times when the head and shoulders of a man appeared at the tailgate of the wagon box. He vaulted over it, hit the ground, and fell over. A second man scrambled belly down over the tailgate and landed atop his companion.

Hobe shot again at the wagon box. This flushed two more men over the tailgate and the driver, perhaps sensing disaster, whipped the team into a tight half-circle that almost tipped the wagon over.

The team was headed for the distant pile of

gear. So were the four men afoot, two of them limping, the fourth dragging a leg and assisted by the third.

"Man, you read that one right," Frank said softly.

As he finished speaking there was a hammering of gunfire from the barn. As Hobe started for the cookshack's door, Marv Freeman knelt, raised his rifle and fired two quick shots. "From the crick," he called. Frank was already at Hobe's post and firing.

Hobe ran between the cookshack benches, around the kitchen and storeroom and swung open the outside door just as a rider galloped past, headed for the barn. Hobe let him ride into his sights and fired. The rider swayed out of his saddle and pitched to the ground. His horse dragged the reins from his hands in an unbroken gallop.

Then there was heavy fire from the bunkhouse and outside of it. Hobe shut the door, slipped the latch and quickly retraced his steps. As he halted in the doorway he saw that all the men save one were kneeling, loading or shooting. The exception was Marv Freeman; he was standing to one side of the door opening on the creek side.

The door he was facing had a slip latch consisting of a peg set in a board that could be slid out of the way. It was, Hobe knew, no kind of lock at all, only a crude bar against the weather outside. Now, whoever was outside knew this, of course. The bar shot back in its slot and the door slammed open. The racket of the gunfire inside drowned out all other sound. Then, with no pretense of caution, Con Jeffries boiled in, a six-gun in each hand.

Marv quickly shot from a distance of four feet. Con took two staggering steps and pitched, face down on the bunkhouse floor, dropping both guns as he fell. Marv stepped over his legs, closed the door and slid the latch.

Bending low, Hobe moved up to Bill Senior's window facing west and looked out. He saw two downed horses and one man lying on his belly. A second man faced the bunkhouse, hands high above his head.

Moving across the room, Hobe came up behind Frank, who was also kneeling to one side of his window. When Frank sensed Hobe's nearness, he looked up and said, "They're on the run, Hobe. Three of them turned and headed for the alders." The firing inside had stopped, so Hobe could hear him add, "I hit one, I think. Leastways he wrapped his arms around his belly and headed for the crick."

Hobe nodded and moved over to the south window and saw three riders approaching the pile of gear and the halted wagon. Hobe moved over to the west door of the bunkhouse and called back into the room, "I'm going out, cover me." He opened the door, moved just outside and looked toward the barn and then at the distant riders.

Afterwards, he moved out toward the tall puncher, who out of sheer weariness had lowered his arms. He stood quietly, not moving, his gun on the ground in front of him. Hobe moved over to him, his rifle dangling from his right hand, and halted, facing the man.

"Go get the wagon and a couple of riders. Then come back here. If any of 'em are packing a gun I'll shoot 'em, but I'll shoot you first."

The puncher tramped off toward the distant wagon and then Hobe went back into the bunkhouse and explained what he had told the puncher. "Stay where you are and keep out of sight," Hobe finished.

Afterwards, he went out and headed for the barn. This, Hobe thought, without any pleasure at all, might teach Lew Seely a prickly lesson. Out of his damned arrogance he had sent at least three men to their deaths, and hurt others. From the beginning this had been a stupid LS move, conceived badly and executed dismally.

Jim and Bates were standing in the doorway of the barn. At their feet was the body of a puncher Jim had knocked off his horse.

As Hobe halted and looked down at the still figure, Jim said, "There's more," and tilted his head toward the corral.

Hobe said tonelessly, "Bates, you get back

into the bunkhouse. They're coming over to pick up their men."

After Bates left for the bunkhouse, Hobe looked out and saw that the puncher was not even halfway to the wagon. "Let's go look," Hobe said to Jim. Together they walked around the side of the corral and came to the gate. A dead man was lying there flat on his back, rope in hand. The flies were already crawling over his face.

"The damn fool," Jim said softly. "When he found the gate wired shut, him and his partner were tryin' to rope the gate posts and drag 'em down."

Hobe noticed that the horses inside the corral were still excited and were bunched as far away from the gate as they could get.

"What about the other one?" Hobe asked.

"Bates nicked him, maybe more. He just run."

Jim took the dead man's lariat, put the loop around one leg, and dragged the body to one side of the gate. Hobe took the wire off the gate, and afterwards both got their saddles out of the stable, caught their horses, and saddled up.

They rode first to the side of the bunkhouse facing the creek, dismounted and went in. They had to step over Con Jeffries, dead on the floor.

Bill Senior was sweeping the broken window glass into a pile in the center of the room. He stopped work, pointed his broom at Jeffries and said, "We'd of dragged him out, only you said don't show outside."

Hobe nodded.

Marv Freeman called from the south window, the only unbroken one, "The wagon's headed this way, with two riders."

"Keep a watch. They won't try the same thing again, but let's make sure." He turned to Jim. "Let's drag him out of here."

"Them horses'll spook, like as not. Bill, you want to be horse-holder?" Jim said.

It took less than a minute for Hobe and Jim to drag out the body. They left it well away from the bunkhouse on the grassy slope, then claimed their nervous horses from Bill and walked them around the bunkhouse.

"You know this country, Jim. Where can they drag the horses where they won't stink us out?"

Jim thought for a moment, then said, "There's a cutbank draw north a ways. Dump 'em in there. Powder'll cave in the banks on 'em." He fisted a hand, extended its thumb and pointed it toward the sky. "It don't take 'em long, does it?"

Hobe looked up at the dozen or so buzzards already circling the high-noon sky, then shook his head.

He looked at the approaching team. The messenger he had sent was seated by the driver. The two riders were closest to the driver as they pulled even with the corner of the bunk-house. Hobe identified the driver as Dad Peters. "Search the lot of them?" Hobe asked.

"Hell, yes. They won't show anything, but slap their boot tops."

Dad reined in the team and Hobe and Jim looked over the two riders and Dad's passenger. All four of them were grim-faced and sullenly angry. Hobe dropped the reins he was holding, walked over to the man seated by Dad, halted, looked up at the puncher and said, "Give them my message?"

The puncher nodded. "Not a gun."

"All right. Face my way and hang your legs over the side."

The young puncher complied and Hobe slapped around the top of each of his boots. He looked at Dad and said, "You do the same, old man." He circled the team and gave Dad's boots the same examination. The two riders, seeing what was expected of them, took their feet out of the stirrups and he checked their boot tops. Afterwards, he backed away and mounted. "We got some dead horses around here," Hobe said to the two mounted men. "If you want their gear, collect it and throw it in the wagon. If you don't want it, then shake out your ropes because you're going to drag your animals off my place."

The two riders looked at each other and one said, "It's a lot of work."

Hobe said, "You brought 'em here, so you

drag 'em off." He tilted his head toward Jim. "He'll show you where to drag 'em. If you see a stray gun around, don't pick it up. It'll get you shot."

Jim raised an arm and pointed to the dead horse out to the west. "Start on that one. I'll be right behind you."

"That's a hell of a waste of money," Dad said. "I could use a new saddle."

"You won't have any trouble findin' it," Jim said. "Just watch the buzzards." To the riders he said, "Get movin'."

The two LS punchers headed for the dead horse and Jim, rifle across his saddle, dropped in behind them.

Hobe asked Dad, "How many men you missin'?"

"Five," Dad said sourly.

"See that dead man by the barn? Load him in the wagon."

Dad drove the wagon over and pulled up alongside the prostrate body. Hobe followed and watched the young puncher swing down from the seat, half-circle the wagon and unhook and lower the tailgate. Then he and Dad loaded the dead man into the wagon.

Afterwards, they picked up the dead man at the corral gate. As they were loading him into the wagon, Hobe glanced over at the distant pile of gear around which men and horses were clustered. The space between the bunkhouse and the distant men was clear. Next

Hobe directed Dad to Con Jeffries' body, behind the bunkhouse. Both hands swore softly and gave Hobe a look of purest hatred. After it was loaded, Hobe said, "Get the wagon across the crick."

Dad drove the team only a short distance before he turned through a break in the alders and crossed the creek. Hobe wasn't sure what they would find, but he crossed well back of the wagon.

On the other side a loose still-saddled horse spooked away. There was a man lying on the ground on his back, one knee bent and jutting up higher than the lush grass. Hobe watched as they loaded the wounded man into the wagon. He was unconscious, but still living and groaning.

The young puncher moved out, caught the horse, brought it back and tied it to the chain of the tailgate. Beyond them, lying face down, was the fifth man. He too was dead. Hobe watched them load him.

Afterwards he rode up on Dad's side of the wagon and reined in. "Tell Seely to keep his men off my place or this'll happen again."

"Tell him yourself," Dad snarled.

Hobe said nothing, only lifted his horse into a canter, heading back for the bunkhouse.

11

Because Stacey was nearest to the front door and Anna was in the kitchen preparing dinner for the three men who took their noon meal and supper there, she answered the door bell. Opening the door, she found Lew Seely facing her.

"Morning, Miss Wheelis. Can I talk to you a minute?"

"Yes, of course." She opened the door wider. "Come in please, Mr. Seely."

As Seely stepped into the dining room, Stacey looked past him and saw the shiny black buggy with driver pulled up to the stepping block.

Seely looked around the dining room and into the adjoining parlor. "You were lucky to get this place. Where did the Gibsons go?"

"With their daughter, Mr. Seely. It turned out to be a little too much for them at their age, they said." She moved past Seely and led the way into the parlor. Sitting down, she watched Seely seat himself in the closest easy chair facing her. He was wearing a gray suit, matching the color of his hair.

He put his black Stetson, crown down, on

the rug and said, "You've cleaned the place up some since the last time I saw it."

"Yes, and it needed it," Stacey said. She wondered at his visit. Why was he here and what did he want of her?

The answer to her questions came after Seely leaned back in his chair, crossed his legs and said, "I'm here on a strange errand, Miss Wheelis. It won't make much sense at first, but I'd like you to think about it."

Stacey only nodded, even more curious.

"My east base camp crew got into a quarrel with a neighbor and his men. It turned into a wide open gunfight between the two crews. Five of my men were killed, four were hurt badly. I brought these four into town to see Dr. Schultz about an hour ago."

"I'm sorry to hear that," Stacey said politely.

"Not as sorry as I am," Seely said grimly. "Dr. Schultz said they shouldn't leave town and that he must see them twice a day. He also said they needed nursing attention."

Stacey was about to protest when Seely raised his hand, palm to her, cutting off the reply he anticipated.

He continued, "As you know, there's no hospital here except the small room off Mrs. Bedloe's even smaller room. She's a nurse, you know."

Stacey frowned. "No, I didn't know."

"Dr. Schultz has no room in his house. Then I remembered hearing that you had taken this place. It occurred to me that if your rooms aren't all rented it would be a good place for my hurt men. Are your rooms rented?"

"No, and I wish they were. But I'm not any kind of a nurse, Mr. Seely. I wouldn't know how to take care of them."

"Of course not," Seely agreed. "That's why I spoke to Mrs. Bedloe about taking a room here. She's willing if you have the room. You'd have nothing to do except give them shelter and feed them. I'd pay anything extra you name, if you would accommodate them."

"If I only have to feed and house them, there'll be no extra charge, Mr. Seely."

"You'll take them, you mean?"

"Why yes, that's my business — room and board."

Seely gave her one of his rare friendly smiles. "I knew I could count on you, and I thank you. Could you show me the rooms?"

Stacey rose and led the way upstairs. She walked to the end of the corridor, opened the door on her left and went inside.

Seely stepped inside, looked around the room and said, "Two beds. Fine."

"All the rooms upstairs have two beds," Stacey said. "Mrs. Gibson said she wanted family trade, people with children."

"Then I'll take three of your rooms, Miss Wheeliss. Two men to a room, and Mrs. Bedloe will have the third. Also, I insist on paying more than your going rate. These men can't

91

help but be a bother to you, even with a nurse." He reached in his hip pocket, drew out a snap purse, counted out five double eagles and handed them to Stacey. "That's to clinch our agreement. Satisfactory to you?"

Was it? Stacey wondered. In a way it was a windfall, but Stacey remembered Anna's loathing of everything related to Seely and LS. She thanked him, saying, "You want to see the other rooms?"

The room across the hall was identical to the one they had just left. The third room, presumably for Mrs. Bedloe, had only a single window; the others had two.

As she led the way down the stairs, Stacey made up her mind to ask a question that had been bothering her since Seely came into the house. In the parlor again, Seely picked up his hat and faced her.

"I don't hear much of the town's talk, Mr. Seely. Just what was the trouble that got five of your men killed and four hurt?"

"A gang of men took over my east line camp. When we tried to take it back, they shot up my crew. I don't know how many there were, because my men saw only two. A man named Carew was the leader and he had an Indian with him."

"I see," Stacey said quietly.

"My men will be brought over in half an hour or so. Thank you again. I hope they won't be too much trouble."

Stacey showed him the door and he shook hands with her before he left.

When Stacey turned to go back to the kitchen she saw Anna standing in the doorway.

"You heard?" Stacey asked.

"Every damn word of it!" Anna said angrily. "You're crazy, Stacey."

"Not as crazy as I'd be turning him down."

Anna moved back into the kitchen, yanked out a chair and sat down. Her black eyes sparkled with anger as she watched Stacey seat herself. "Now, explain what you just said." Her voice still held harsh anger.

Stacey's reply held no anger at all. "All right. You can bet he knows our rooms are empty. That's likely why he came here. What if I'd said we couldn't take his men? Wouldn't he wonder why?"

"That's your business only!"

"No. He'd make it his business to find out. He was kind enough to help me and he knows we need money, but I won't help him. Why?"

"It's still your business."

"*Think,* Anna. He'd send a man straight to Riverbend because that's where my bank draft came from. His man would go to Marshal Hood first, because it was Hood that wrote Sheriff Inglish to cancel my pick-up. Hood would tell him about Hobe and me." She shrugged. "Now I've done him a favor, he won't send a man downriver. Don't you see?"

"Yes, you're right and I'm wrong," Anna said slowly, her anger gone. Then she added dryly, "I hope the good Lord keeps me from shooting our new boarders while they're sleeping."

Stacey shivered without being aware of it. "It sounds like our menfolk are taking care of that. Do you think they're hurt?"

"They'd be quicker to tell us than Lew Seely did. No, I don't think they're hurt."

The door bell clanged and Stacey rose. "I'll answer it. You stay out of sight. My guess it'll be Mrs. Bedloe. She's got to be coming."

Stacey opened the door to a plump, gray-haired woman who introduced herself as the new nurse. Behind her was an LS hand, the buggy driver, and he had two suitcases in his hands.

Stacey showed Mrs. Bedloe her room, the driver left, and Stacey returned to the kitchen. Anna was busy with dinner for their three boarders and the four men coming. Stacey joined her at the counter as Anna said, "I've been thinking. Hobe and Jim can walk in here anytime and be recognized by one of the hurt men. That would do it, wouldn't it?"

"Yes, but they'll be in their rooms."

"I know an Indian boy here who'd ride out with it tomorrow. He knows where the Parry place is. Another thing," she paused and looked at Stacey, "from the time these saddle bums get here I'm just a dumb, halfwit Indian squaw. I don't really understand white man's talk and don't speak it too good." She smiled. "That way I won't have to talk to them and maybe I can overhear stuff."

"Anna, you think of everything."

"I didn't a little while ago," Anna said wryly.

The door bell clanged and Stacey said, "Well, here they are," and headed for the front door.

When they heard footsteps at the doorway that were coming closer, both Sheriff Inglish and his deputy looked up. Lew Seely came into the office, waved a careless greeting to them and took off his hat.

"Get lost, Ed," the sheriff said.

Ed Humbolt rose obediently and headed for the door. Without looking at him, Seely passed him and headed for the deputy's chair. Ed closed the door behind him. Seely tossed his hat on the desk and sat down in Ed's chair, facing Inglish.

"How much have you heard?" Seely asked.

"All of it, I reckon. I, talked with your man while you were in Doc's office."

"I want you to move them off, Burt."

As if he hadn't heard, Inglish went on, "I saw Parry, then. Yes, he sold his place to Carew. It's even recorded in the clerk's office down the hall, Lew."

"I want you to move them off," Seely repeated.

The sheriff eyed him calmly. "I can't, and you damned well know I can't, Lew. If he'd kept

95

your horses I could move against him, but he never."

"I built the bunkhouse. It's mine."

"Then move it off, if you can," Inglish said dryly. "You can't because it's adobe. Besides you'd be trespassin' without his permission."

"Nobody can do this to me," Seely flared. "Why do you think I bought your election?"

"Not to get me killed!" Inglish said angrily. "Say I deputized thirty men and tried to move Carew off. The same thing that happened to you would happen to me. More than that. On any dark night I could get shot in the back. If I try to take Carew's property away from him it means I'll try it on anybody. I'm dead."

"Politically, you're dead right now!"

"Along with you if I start rememberin' things and talk."

Seely looked at him for moments, then smiled. "Why are we growling at each other, Burt? You're right, of course. It's just that I hate losing something I counted as mine." He added as an afterthought, "And the men, of course. That goes without saying."

Inglish nodded. "Who wants to lose? Sometimes you got to, but you don't have to like it."

If there was irony in Burt's words and tone of voice Seely couldn't detect it. The sheriff's gray eyes seemed troubled, as if in sympathy. *It's easy to feel sorry for a loser when you're a winner,* Seely thought sourly.

He rose and picked up his hat. "There could

96

be gunplay out our way, Burt. Expect it."

"So long as I don't see it, I don't know who started or who to believe, do I?"

"I think you do."

Burt smiled thinly. "I think so too."

12

As the twelve-year-old Indian boy approached the LS line camp on his pony he wondered what had happened to the place since he'd last seen it with Jim. The windows of the bunkhouse were gone, their frames splintered, and the face of the adobe building looked as if it had been hacked all over with a pick-ax. In fact, he was certain the place was abandoned and Anna didn't know it.

And then Bates appeared in the bunkhouse doorway, hands on hips. As the boy approached, Bates waved and called, "Hi, Joey."

Joey waved and rode closer and reined up before Bates. "What's happened here, Mr. Jordan? Where's everybody?"

"You mean the word ain't reached town yet?"

"Oh, the LS fight. I knew it happened. I didn't hear where."

"Right here, Joey. Now, light and eat. You gotta be hungry."

Joey swung down, reached inside his shirt and pulled out a letter and handed it to Bates.

" 'Fore I forget it, Anna said to give this to Jim. He here?"

"Nope. He could be anywhere but here right now. I'll see he gets it."

Hobe handed Jim the binoculars, saying, "Look what's in the wagon."

They were on the timbered ridge above and to the east of LS headquarters ranch, just above the big house. Just to the south of it was a huge pond, almost a lake. The stream that fed it from the north was bridged for the road to the bunkhouse and corrals.

Jim was glassing the team and wagon coming from the north and he was silent for several moments, then said, "Coffins, and a preacher beside the driver. I don't believe it."

"Time to go? The crew'll be afoot," Hobe said.

"Just right."

Jim led the way back and over the ridge to the waiting horses and the pack horse. Careful not to skyline themselves, they moved south until they had lost the lake and then Jim led the way down through the timber to the stream, then turned back north.

They pulled up, still in the timber, where the rock-lined spillway in the earth dam funneled the lake's water back into a stream. Both men went back to the pack horse, whose only pack was a big *aparejo* of heavy canvas, a deep pocket on each side. From these pockets they took a short-handled shovel, pry bars, and canvas sacks of Giant powder with fuse cord.

As they tramped back toward the noisy outlet whose tumbling waters would drown out speech, Jim asked, "We take turns on lookout?"

"Don't think we'll have to," Hobe answered. "They'll be too busy."

They swung down into the rocky creekbed and Hobe, leading the way, climbed up the sloping back of the dam until he could look through the V of the spillway takeoff. Then they started digging below the lake's level and slanting down toward it. It was hard, awkward work in the now-fading light. When they were in as far as they could go they placed the charges, trailed out the long line of fuse cord and faced each other.

Hobe said then, "Find a low spot in the creekbank, Jim. When we get out of here it'll be in a hell of a hurry. Leave the tools. They're theirs anyway."

Jim left in the lowering dusk. When Hobe heard his low whistle he knelt by the end of the fuse cord, struck a match, touched it to the cord, waited until it began to sputter sparks, then rose and ran for Jim at the creekbank. Both of them headed up the steep draw, made the timber and halted, waiting.

Presently, the earth jarred beneath them and there was a sudden brightness, then they heard the blast of the explosion. Rocks and dirt pelted down through the trees.

The sound of water funneling down the spill-way changed its tone into a growling rock-clat-tering roar that slowly increased in volume as freed water sawed through the break. They moved toward the creek in time to see the foaming crest of a wave as high as the bank pass ahead of them.

"They'll come around the end of the lake. We better git," Jim said.

They found their horses and angled south and up the ridge. As they crested it they heard the instant tumble of an explosion from the mountain to the west.

"Well, there goes a crick buried," Jim said. "Wonder when Seely'll start haulin' water?"

On the heels of his words the rifle fire started on two sides of the big house, breaking a window with each shot. They looked at the scene below. A coffin lay beside each grave, ready for burial. What crew remained was in the corral trying to rope a mount in the fading light.

"Why are they botherin'?" Jim asked, deri-sion in his voice. "By the time they're saddled it'll be too dark to pick up signs."

Jim looked at the lake. Already its shoreline was receding, exposing mud flats. Water was churning at the new outlet they had blown, widening it with each passing minute.

"Good night and sweet dreams, Mr. Seely," Hobe said dryly. He wheeled his horse and

Jim and the pack horse fell in beside him.

Heading east, Hobe felt a wicked satisfaction. Out of a carefully cultivated sense of power with its inevitable arrogance, neither Seely nor his crew believed LS headquarters could be, or would be attacked. Proof was that no guards had been posted on the logical sentinel spots to give warning of the approach of strangers. The arrival of the coffins and their unloading and sealing the dead men in was a lucky diversion, but the plan would have worked without it. LS had been caught with its guard down. *So far,* Hobe thought with reflective caution.

They arrived at the east base camp after midnight and there was no lamplight visible. Hobe called, "Hello the house! It's me and Jim."

There was the briefest silence and then Bates answered from the bunkhouse, "Sing out, Jim."

"Just the two of us, Bates."

By lantern light they unsaddled in the corral, fed their horses, then headed for the now-lamplit bunkhouse.

Bates had two places set at the table nearest the kitchen and as they wearily sat down, he came in from the kitchen with a platter of sizzling steaks and steaming potatoes. Sitting with the food between them, he said to Jim, "Joey brought out a letter from your wife this mornin', Jim. It's under your plate."

101

Jim found the letter, said to Hobe, "Go ahead and eat," and, ignoring the food, opened the letter and began reading it. Hobe helped himself to the food, and was eating when he heard Jim say softly, "Well, I'll be damned." Finished, he put the letter beside his plate and, scowling, helped himself to the food. Both hungry men ate in silence while Bates joined them with his cup of coffee. All three men wanted to talk and ask questions, but they all kept silent. Hobe drained his coffee cup and shoved his plate aside. Seeing him, Jim flipped the letter before him, but it was to Bates he spoke.

"Bates, you know where we went today? What we did?"

"No notion," Bates said cheerfully.

"You won't, either. You won't know what's in that letter, either. You know why?"

"Sure. You're trying to keep LS off my back. What I don't know they can't beat out of me — them or the sheriff."

"That's right, old friend. You never asked for any part of this. We made you stay because we had to have a cook. We paid you, so what the hell was the difference. You knew me and Hobe from before. No other names. Make up front names if they ask. Brands you don't read good. Besides, you never paid attention or wasn't close enough to see 'em. You —"

Bates held up his hand, palm out, interrupting, "I know, I know."

102

"Then will you kindly leave us the hell alone," Jim said, grinning. "We got business that's none of yours."

All three men laughed and Bates rose, the other two with him, and they cleared the table. Afterwards, Hobe and Jim came back to the table and Bates shut the door behind them.

Hobe read the letter and then, like Jim, read it again, not because it was unclear but because its news was difficult to immediately take in. "Well, I'll be damned, too." He flipped the letter back to Jim.

"That little Stacey thinks quick," Jim said.

Hobe nodded. "Instinct for survival, maybe."

"But quick and right, like Anna says." He thought for a moment, then asked, "You guessin' what happens next?"

"Kind of. You are too." Hobe yawned vastly. "Let's chew it over tomorrow when we're both awake."

Hobe blew the lamp and both weary men sought their bunks and said good night. In the darkness he thought again of Anna's letter. Two defenseless women were sleeping under the same roof as four of the enemy crew. An overheard conversation or a slip of the tongue reported to Seely would bring swift reprisal on the women. They were atop a powder keg, but they knew it. They would be careful, he knew; they *had* to be.

13

Sheriff Inglish was mad. He was mad at being roused before daylight and at the cold, hurried breakfast he had had to wolf down. He'd been especially mad at the taciturn LS hand who'd refused to tell him why he was being summoned.

"He said to tell you nothin'. He wants you to see for yourself." The 'he,' of course, was Lew Seely.

"See what?"

"You'll see."

"Goddamnit, I've got a deputy! That is what I pay him for! Go get *him!*"

"He said you."

This had been the last exchange between them. The sharp edge of his anger had finally worn off during the long ride, to be replaced by caution. Recalling his argument of yesterday with Lew over his refusal to arrest Carew, he knew he had barely won that one. He also knew he couldn't afford to anger Lew further. The thing to do was to accommodate Lew in every way until his favors cancelled his insubordination. Otherwise Lew would back another man in the fall election.

It was a sunny midday when they approached the big house. His silent companion headed straight for the office at the west end on the wing. Alert and observant, the sheriff noted the shattered windows along the building. The puncher halted his horse at the office doorway.

And then the sheriff saw it and asked in slow shock, "Where's the lake?"

"Downstream, I reckon," the puncher said dryly.

The sheriff put his horse forward and reined up past the corner of the office for a closer look. He could not believe his eyes. Save for a puddle of water maybe four feet in circumference in the center of a vast and already stinking mud flat, there was no lake. A broad trench in the mud led to the southeast corner of the mud flat where there was no longer any dam.

The sheriff pulled his horse around and headed back for the office. The puncher was gone and Lew Seely, wearing Levis and denim jacket, stood in the office doorway. His lean face was drawn and unshaved.

The sheriff faced him, nodded toward the mud flats and said, "Who and what done that?"

"You've got to ask?" Seely said sarcastically.

"I been askin' why you wanted me since I was woke up this mornin' and I ain't had an answer yet. Let's have one now."

"Why, Carew blew a hole in the dam," Seely

said bitterly. "Notice anything else?"

"Should I have?"

"There's no water coming in. They blew the springs that fed it, too." He tilted his hand toward the office. "Come in."

Seely slacked wearily into the corner of the sofa nearest his desk. Inglish took the middle of the same sofa, put his elbows on knees, looked at Seely and said, "Tell me all of it."

Seely did. When the dam blew up the men were getting ropes ready to lower the coffins into the graves. Nobody knew what to do. Keyhoe then ordered them to saddle up. Then the second explosion came and the sniping began.

"Where were you?"

"Outside at first. Then I came back here to get out of the sniper fire. I lay down on the floor in broken glass."

"Anybody see 'em?"

"Nobody saw anybody. It was getting dark." He paused. "Now you know all I know."

"But how do you know it was Carew's bunch?"

"Who in hell else would it be?" Seely demanded angrily, leaning forward. "Burt, I want that Carew gang rounded up and arrested — every man! I'll sign a complaint charging them with attempted murder and malicious destruction of property! I want it done today!"

The sheriff had his mouth open to say something in protest, changed his mind, stood up and said, "It wouldn't hurt to talk to 'em. Let's go."

14

Bates put down the binoculars, moved to the paneless window, looked out at the barn and whistled piercingly. Hobe and Jim appeared almost instantly, each with a rifle in hand, and dog-trotted toward the bunkhouse, Jim looking west, Hobe east.

They hauled up before Bates standing in the doorway.

"Make 'em out?" Hobe asked.

Bates handed him the binoculars. "Can't be sure. Lost 'em in the trees, but I reckon it's Sheriff Inglish and the commissioner hisself."

Hobe took the glasses and looked through them for long moments, then grunted. He handed the glasses to Jim and said, "Bates, you get back in the kitchen. They'll want to talk to you, but make 'em call you."

Bates disappeared. Jim seated himself in the doorway and Hobe put a shoulder against the sun-warm walls. Neither spoke, since they were fairly sure of what was going to be said.

The buckboard came out of the trees, and headed for the bunkhouse, the sheriff at the reins. When it was well short of the bunkhouse the sheriff reined in and called, "Want to talk to you two. Come on over."

Hobe called, "Can't hear you. Come closer."

The sheriff swore softly, put the horse in motion, made a half-circle and pulled up before the bunkhouse door. Each pair of men regarded the other with quiet hostility.

"Want to talk to you two," the sheriff repeated.

"We figured you did," Hobe answered.

"Why?" the sheriff asked swiftly.

"Well, you wouldn't drive all this way just to look at us, I reckon."

The sheriff glanced at Seely. So did Hobe and Jim. They saw the anger reflected in his beard-stubbled, tired face. The sight of it must have angered the sheriff too, for he turned to face them again. There was a ferocious scowl on his hound's face.

"What do you two know about the headquarters ranch being wrecked?"

"Lots," Hobe said. "Anything in particular?"

"Yes. Who blew the dam?"

Hobe tilted his head toward Jim, still seated. "We did."

"Who blew the springs? Who shot up the house?"

"My crew."

"And who's your crew? Give me names."

"Find out. You're the sheriff," Hobe said calmly.

"That's withholdin' criminal information. You're under arrest on that charge. You're under arrest on two other charges — attempted murder is one. Malicious destruction of property while trespassin' is another."

Hobe gave him a slow smile, looked briefly at Seely's stony expression, then asked, "Sheriff, have you also arrested the man sitting beside you?"

Seely spoke for the first time, and coldly. "No, he hasn't. On what charges would he have grounds for arresting me?"

"Exactly the same grounds he has for arresting me," Hobe countered. "Withholding criminal information. Did you tell him you sent Con Jeffries to kick me off my place? Attempted murder. Do you think your men used slingshots to break my windows or scar up the buildings? Malicious destruction of property while trespassing? Look around you again."

Hobe shifted his glance to the sheriff. "Well, Sheriff? You arrest both of us or neither of us. Which will it be?"

"It's you alone, by God!" Inglish exploded.

Jim lifted his rifle, cocking it as he did so. "Who started it — him or us?"

"You think blowing up a dam and cutting off all the water is like shootin' at a 'dobe bunkhouse? You think —"

"I know Seely started it," Jim broke in roughly. "He started it back on Silver Creek and started it again here."

"You're both resistin' arrest. That's another charge."

Jim lifted the barrel of his rifle a little higher and said softly, "If you don't get the hurry-hell out of here, you'll find out how we resist arrest."

Oddly, the expression on the sheriff's face was one of relief. His gray eyes held a hint of suppressed amusement. He didn't even look at Seely as he slapped the reins and put the buckboard in motion. He had said all the things and made all the moves that Seely expected of him, and it had turned out exactly as he had known it would.

Bates opened the door and joined them and as they watched the buckboard diminish in the distance Bates said, "I wouldn't 'a missed that for all the whiskey in Two Rivers." He looked from Jim to Hobe. "What I'm wonderin' is where do you go from here?"

"Not to any jail," Hobe said grimly.

15

On the fourth day of their hospitalization Dr. Schultz gave permission to two of the hurt LS hands to dress and move around. Since there was very little moving-around space in the upstairs rooms, Nurse Bedloe asked Stacey if her two patients could use the parlor downstairs.

"Their rent's been paid and the parlor's part of it. Of course," Stacey answered. This took place after the doctor's morning visit. Within minutes, two of the hurt men were downstairs and in the parlor. When Stacey looked in on them a parlor table had been moved to the center of the room, two dining-room chairs had been appropriated and a card game was in progress. They were both wearing their hats, as they would in any saloon card game.

When Anna had taken their dinners up to the two men upstairs, the regular boarders began to arrive for the noon meal. They were all young, store clerks or bookkeepers, mild, pleasant men.

Stacey came to the parlor door and said, "Dinner's on." The men started for the dining room; seeing that the two LS hands still wore their hats she added, "No hats at the table, please."

"What about women?" This, from the tallest and burliest of the two LS hands.

"They can, but you don't look like a woman."

"I'm paid for. I'll wear what I damn please."

"In the barn, yes." She turned to Anna. "Anna, will you please serve our guest in the barn?"

Anna caught on immediately, and with relish and sullen mock-Indian dignity she said, "Me paid to work in house, not in barn. I hold

111

back door open, yes."

The LS man looked with hatred at the two women and said, "The hell with it," took off his Stetson and threw it, with his good arm, toward a parlor chair. The other arm was bandaged, wrist to elbow. His partner, watching, did the same.

In the kitchen, after they had had their quiet laugh, they ate their dinner, taking turns with the coffee pot and water pitcher, tending their boarders' wants. When Anna went into the dining room on her turn Stacey again had the thought she hadn't discussed with Anna. With half the patients up and moving the situation here was different; it would be even more so when the bedridden pair were able to come downstairs. There would be four idle, restless men penned up in the house and under foot all day, probably visitors who would bring bottles to cheer up the sick, the parlor would be smoke-thick and, of course, a marathon card game would almost always be in progress.

Should she talk it over with Anna, warn her? *No, she's twice my age, and twice as smart. She'll know without my saying it,* Stacey thought.

Dinner finished, the boarders gone and the dishes done, Stacey threw on a light shawl, put on a wide brimmed straw hat, pocketed her grocery list and headed for the front door. The same two LS hands had resumed their card game, their hats on again.

Anna, tired from her morning's chores, passed through the parlor, ignoring the two men, went into her tiny room, closed the door and lay down on her bed.

A half-hour later, her errands done, Stacey returned home. The parlor was empty, the house quiet. Stacey crossed the dining room, opened the kitchen door and halted abruptly.

Anna, seated in one of the kitchen chairs, had a cocked six-gun in her hand and it was pointed at Stacey. When Anna saw Stacey she lowered the gun and took it off cock.

"Anna, what on earth!" Stacey came toward her. "Why were you pointing that gun at me?"

"Not at you, Stacey. I was expecting another call from our overfriendly boarder, the one we made fun of this noon."

Stacey moved closer. "Your cheek is cut and swollen. What happened, Anna?"

Anna told her of going to her room for a nap. She was wakened by the movement of the bed just before her wrists were pinned to the bed. When she started to cry out she was brutally cuffed into silence. And then he started to feel under her skirts, her breasts, her whole body, all the time talking.

"I thought I'd heard all the dirty words ever made up, but I was wrong. All of them were meant to cajole a stupid Indian bitch into spreading her legs. Then he lay on me. I got in a kick in his crotch and a good one. That's when I got this." She touched her cut cheek. "Then I went for his hurt arm, pounding on it. He had to roll off me and that's when I took his gun that he'd taken off."

Stacey moved to her, put her arms around Anna's shoulders and hugged her. "Didn't you call for help?"

"So his friend would come down and hold me while he got what he wanted? No."

"Oh it's all my fault, Anna — my fault, alone. I should never have taken them in." Stacey's voice was gentle, but inside she felt an anger that was nearly overwhelming. This was a time of all times when they needed a man, and both their men were gone, probably on the run. And then Stacey came to her angry decision.

"Anna, what's that brute's name?"

"His bottle of medicine says Fred Norton on the label. Why?"

"He's not going to get away with it," Stacey said evenly. "I'm going to the law with this. Do you care?"

Anna smiled painfully. "I care a lot — that you do go."

"It won't be any fun when they talk to you."

"Neither was that any fun."

"Then you stay right here. Don't clean up. I want them to see you. Just wait for me."

Stacey went out the back door and headed for the courthouse, walking swiftly, sometimes running, indifferent to the curious stares of the people on the street.

At the courthouse she was directed to the office of Sheriff Inglish. Entering the room, she saw that the chair behind the biggest desk was unoccupied, but pudgy Ed Humbolt sat in his. He smiled at the sight of this pretty girl, started to rise, then remembered he was the authority here and remained seated.

As Stacey halted before him he asked, "What can I do for you, Miss —"

"My name is Stacey Wheeliss. I run the new boarding house the Gibsons used to own. I'd like to talk with Sheriff Inglish."

"He's out of town, Miss Wheeliss. I'm his deputy. You can talk with me, or wait for him."

"This can't wait," she hesitated, then plunged on, "I want to report an attempted rape."

Ed's button mouth briefly sagged open and his face flushed. "An attempt on you?" he asked angrily.

"No, no. I'm not saying this right." She paused to reflect. "On my housekeeper and friend, Mrs. Byers." She went on to relate Anna's brief account of what took place while Stacey had been out. As she talked she saw that the deputy was fast losing interest.

When she was finished, Ed asked idly, "Any witnesses?"

"To a rape? Are there ever?"

Ed shrugged, but at the same time he was

shaking his head. "That's an old story, Miss Wheeliss. A woman teases a man until he loses his head and goes for her. Then she claims he attacked her. Most squaws settle for a pint of whiskey, even if what they say is true. You said she was Indian, didn't you?"

Stacey felt a helpless rage. This fool was equating Anna with the derelict Indians the whiskey traders preyed on. But she knew any further show of temper would only prejudice him more deeply.

"She's not that sort," Stacey said quietly. "I believe her, if you don't. Still, that doesn't change things. She works for me. She lives in my house and was beat up by one of my boarders. If that doesn't call for an arrest, what does?"

"What's his name? Who is he?"

"An LS hand, name of Fred Norton. I won't have him in my place any longer, but he's too big for me to throw out. I can shoot him, though, but that would make me as bad as him."

Humbolt smiled — why, Stacey didn't know. He rose, said, "Let's go," and motioned toward the doorway.

There was a buckboard already hitched in the wagon shed and Humbolt handed Stacey up and climbed up beside her. As they drove out into the street Humbolt said, "You come to the wrong office, Miss Wheeliss, but it don't really matter. You should have gone to the

116

marshal, but he's deputized us and we deputized him, so I'll do."

At her house, Stacey led the way into the kitchen. Anna was seated where Stacey had left her. Her face was swollen more and its cut was still bleeding.

Humbolt looked at her with distaste and open contempt. Hands on fat hips, he faced Anna. "What's your story?" he asked with feigned patience.

Anna told him. When she was finished he looked at Stacey and asked, "Where is he?"

Stacey gave him directions and he turned toward the kitchen door.

"Do I sign something?" Anna asked.

"At the marshal's office," Humbolt said over his shoulder as he left the kitchen.

Anna went over to the sink, took down a basin and filled it with water. Watching her, Stacey said, "Anna, don't expect anything to come of this."

Anna smiled crookedly, "You think I was? No. Whatever I sign will wind up in the wastebasket before I'm out the door."

They both fell silent as they heard the stumbling racket on the stairs. That would be Humbolt helping Norton to navigate, possibly with the help of Nurse Bedloe. The racket ended and Humbolt appeared in the kitchen doorway, Norton's warbag dangling from one hand.

"He says he has some money comin' to him,"

the deputy announced. "And his gun's missin'."

Stacey moved to the table, picked up the gun and gave it to Humbolt, then went past him into the dining room. Norton, hat on, stood by the door, a sullen anger on his face.

"I don't owe you money. I owe it to Mr. Seely. Now get out of here and don't come back! Not even to visit your friends!"

When the two men had left Stacey returned to the kitchen where Anna was gently washing her swollen face.

"I forgot to ask the deputy where he was taking Norton. Dr. Schultz will want to know."

"The drunk cell at the jail. He'll know. They never lock it on a white man." Anna didn't look up from soaping her washcloth.

"What does that mean?"

"That the doctor doesn't have to hunt up a deputy to let him in."

"You mean more than that," Stacey said quietly.

The two women looked at each other. "I mean they'd lock up an Indian. After he was sentenced, he'd be put to work on roads or bridges until he'd worked off his fine."

Stacey was silent for a moment, then said quietly, "My God, how can you live with us?"

"Sometimes it takes some doing. Then I remember Jim's half-white and his father was a good man. And who helped me today? It was a white girl, wasn't it?"

16

The two LS hands and Dana Keyhoe were waiting in his office when Lew Seely came in from the windy, cold June morning. Dana rose even as Seely moved toward his desk with a curt nod to the three men.

As soon as Seely was seated at his desk, Keyhoe came forward and put two checks before him. "These men want their time, Lew," Dana said. "They're quittin'."

Seely looked past Dana to the two punchers. "Why you quitting? I pay better wages than other outfits."

The two hands looked at each other and the taller puncher answered first. "I'm a natural-born fiddlefoot. Want to see some new country."

"Me too," the second said quickly.

Seely smiled. "Now you've got that out of the way, what's the real reason? Sit down and tell me."

Reluctantly, the two men sat down on the handiest sofa, Dana sat opposite them. Before anyone else could speak, Seely asked pleasantly, "Getting a little too hot in the kitchen for you fellows?"

Seely's looks had changed. He knew it, and he knew they knew it. From a healthy and handsome leanness, both his body and face were almost gaunt.

The taller puncher nodded. "Ain't what we hired on for, boss. Close as I can figure it, we're shorthanded and gittin' shorter. I don't figger to spend the whole damn summer behind a plow or with a shovel in my hands or stretchin' wire. They'll start it all over again afore we're done."

Too damned true, Seely thought bitterly. He said, "We're pulling our men in. We'll have help."

"What happens to what you pull 'em off of?" the smaller puncher asked. "Line shacks burned. I don't like buildin' 'em."

"We're hiring," Dana said.

"Not me."

"Not me neither," the other puncher said.

Resignedly, Seely pulled the checks toward him and countersigned them. Dana handed them to the two men, who had already risen.

As they were pocketing them Seely said, "Good luck, boys, but don't come back."

"Don't look like there'll be much left to come back to," the short puncher observed.

They shook hands with Keyhoe and left. Dana came back to his seat. Seely was looking out the window at the swarm of men and horses working with wagons and stoneboats at the gaping wedge that powder and water had created. If the coffer dam they'd thrown up could hold back the water they might, just might, complete the job. He felt a deep and black discouragement as he looked at Dana, who was suppressing an expression that matched Seely's.

"Two more gone. How does this end, Dana?"

"More pay'll keep 'em, maybe bring some, though God knows it's high enough now."

"I wasn't thinking of that." He nodded toward the dam. "The whole thing, I mean. We're in a war, Dana. How do we end it? Send for the U.S. Marshal?"

"That's the last thing you've ever wanted. The U.S Commissioner damn well knows it and so do his men."

"I know, I know, but this is turning into Civil War of sorts."

"But we started it, like the sheriff says. We ask for help and that 'opens the ball.' We'd be in court for years. You know that and so do I, and we'd lose."

"Then what do we do?"

Keyhoe had never been asked this question before; he'd asked the questions and been told what to do. Now the almighty boss was *asking* him, not telling him. The temptation to seize only a fraction of power was almost irresistible, but Keyhoe knew his man. It would never be forgiven.

"Why, stomp 'em like you always have," he

said. "Once we get caught up here, then hunt 'em down."

"Who do we hunt outside of Carew and that damned Indian? How many are there and who are they?"

"Nobody's sure. When we hit Parry's the boys said fifteen or twenty. Nobody saw a man besides the two."

"Think back. Who've we chased off that would fight?"

"Can't tell. Why didn't they fight back when we ran them off?"

"Carew," Seely said glumly.

Keyhoe sighed and rose. "Well, this ain't gettin' a dam repaired. See you later."

After Keyhoe went out, Seely leaned back in his chair, hands hooding the tips of the chair arms, head lowered. He had never experienced this feeling of helplessness before and he hated it.

Was it only a week or so back that he was truly the ruler of this range? Any LS rider was feared and with good cause. Any move against LS or its crew brought instant and savage retaliation. Yet in a matter of days he'd lost the upper hand. Five of his men were dead, four in the hospital, and his own sheriff was powerless to help him. His crew, slowly but surely, was deserting him. Here he was cowering in his house on a little patch of land while a bunch of marauding riffraff ravaged his property.

A slow anger began to heat up in him. Why was he accepting this instead of fighting back? To attack and destroy Parry's old place, the east line camp, was senseless, as had been proved. What he wanted was Carew and that Indian, obviously the leaders of that bunch. Get them, and the others would cut and run. How could they be found, though?

Suddenly he sat upright. Why hunt them? Let them hang themselves. It would cost a couple of LS hands, but it would net those two.

Thinking closely, he concluded that this was something he had to do himself. He wouldn't even trust Keyhoe with it, since it must be known by only two men, and he, himself, was one of them.

He rose, went to the wall safe behind his desk, dialed it open and took out an envelope containing a thick sheaf of banknotes, all twenties, all used, all untraceable. From his office closet he took down his hat and denim jacket, put them on and left for the corral. Ordinarily, he would have ordered his horse saddled and brought to the door, but not today. No man could be spared from the work on the dam.

Once saddled up, he headed south. With each mile he traveled he became more certain that he had chosen the right man for this job. Will Musick — not his real name — was a renegade Texas Ranger. His Mexican wife had cuckolded him. After beating her and putting her in the hospital he had opened a personal vendetta against all Spanish-Americans and Indians. Two wholly unnecessary killings had resulted in his dismissal with prejudice.

He had arrived in Two Rivers with a new name, a friend and a small band of good horses, liked what he saw and decided to settle there. Seely had looked at his stock and had loaned him money to buy a small place against the Dexters, where the summer graze was good.

Two months later a detective employed by the Texas Cattleman's Association had called on him at the bank. He was after a certain Tom Sauers, a talented horsethief who was reported headed this way. His description of Sauers fitted Will Musick to a hair.

Seely, on impulse, had shaken his head. "Doesn't ring a bell with me, but ask around town. Be here long?"

"Depends," the detective had said.

"We're busy for the next couple of days with end-of-the-month billing. After that, you're welcome to look at our books. With an employee watching, of course." He had smiled then. "No offense meant, but we have to guard our paper like we do our money."

The detective had left and not returned. *Money in the bank,* Seely had thought later. He had a real pry on Musick. He was on his way now to using it.

Musick's Flying M was little more than a log

cabin and barn abutting a corral and big horse pasture. There was a racket of blacksmithing coming from the near corner of the barn and Seely headed for it. Dismounting, he went through an end door of the barn and found himself in a small room separated from the barn's runway by a shoulder-high partition. Working at the forge was a big half-bald man in his middle thirties who saw Seely's shadow and looked up. He smiled then and said, "Hi, Mr. Seely. You're a long ways from that bank of yours."

"Like to talk with you if you can spare a minute, Musick."

"Sure thing." He looked at the forge. "Little hot in here. Why don't we hunt up some shade outside?"

Musick led the way around the end of the barn to a shady spot, then both men sat down, their backs against the barn logs.

"What brings you out this way?" Musick asked.

"A talented horsethief named Sauers, Tom," Seely said, watching him. "I'm quoting a Cattle Association detective."

Musick looked at him impassively. He finally asked, "How long've you known?"

"A couple of months."

"Why the wait?"

"I figured I could use you sometime. The time's here."

"Time to call in the mortgage? Time to turn

me over to the law? Time to claim my breedin' stock?"

"None of those," Seely answered. "Time I paid you to stir up a ruckus in Two Rivers and come back here. Nothing will change except you'll be richer."

"What kind of ruckus?"

Seely told him, paid him, shook hands and rode out. Musick watched him go, then looked at his hand, swore, wiped it on his pants and then turned and headed for the house.

Next day Musick got to Two Rivers about dusk. He ate a hasty meal, easily found Stacey's boarding house, took down his warbag stuffed with paper, tied his horse and knocked on the door. It was answered by Anna, who told him yes, they did have an empty room.

The parlor was deserted, but the lamps were lighted. Musick paid for two nights, registered as John Smith, then followed Anna upstairs and was shown his room. He threw his warbag on the chair and said, "I'll be goin' out again. Can you leave the door unlocked?"

Anna said she could and left the room. Musick listened to her go down the steps and into the kitchen. Opening the door, he heard male voices in conversation in the end room, whose door was open. This was the room Seely had described.

Drawing his gun, he walked softly down the

hall and halted in the doorway of the room. One man was lying on the left bed, talking to the second man, sitting on the opposite bed.

"You lost or somethin'?" the prone man asked of Musick.

Musick lifted his gun and shot him. The second man lunged for his gun and shellbelt draped over the footboard of his bed.

Musick shot again and heard the raw grunt of driven breath.

Musick wheeled and ran for the stairs. He took them two at a time and at the bottom skirted the dining tables, wrenched open the door, leaped down the steps and reached his waiting horse. There were shouts from inside, but he vaulted into the saddle, put his horse into a walk and rode off into the night.

He'd done the job he'd been paid for, but he didn't like any part of it. What kind of a son of a bitch would pay to have two of his own crew bushwhacked?

17

"This time you arrest him, by the Lord Harry, or you turn in your badge," Seely said angrily.

"But you don't know it was him. The Injun woman's description don't fit him," the sheriff protested.

Seely rose from his chair in front of the

sheriff's desk and began to pace. "You can bet it'll fit one of his gang! Who else would be gunning for my crew? You don't even know who they are, but you know who's their leader. Are you afraid of Carew?"

"Hell yes, I am."

"You are also stupid," Seely countered. "Can't you see the difference between this and the last time we talked with him? Then he was getting even with me for destroying his property. But this time it's plain calculated murder! No property rights involved on either side. Just plain murder!"

"It was a hell of a thing," the sheriff agreed.

"That's not good enough, Burt, and you know it! You've got a lawless gang in this county that won't stop at unprovoked murder. You know the leaders — Carew and his Indian. What's the excuse for any lawman if he can't stop that? Come to that, what's the excuse for any law?"

"It'll call for a big posse, and that costs money."

"So what do we pay taxes for if it isn't protection of life and limb, first of all?" He sat down again. "What did Harbison say? If he's the district attorney, he's the one to get this rolling."

"When I come in, he was out. I left word for him. I can't move without his sayin' to."

"You could be rounding up possemen."

"Not till he authorizes me."

128

Seely stood up. "Leave word at the bank. If I don't get fast action on this, tell Harbison two can play this game of bushwhack and I'm willing to play it."

Hobe, working in the corral, heard the team approach. He went through the stable into the barn and then headed for the bunkhouse. There was a buckboard and team pulled up before it and Sheriff Inglish was just climbing down. When he saw Hobe he pulled a paper from his hip pocket. His passenger, a bespectacled young man dressed in a dark townsman's suit, climbed down on his side.

The three men met by the buckboard's rear wheel. "Carew, this here's Mel Harbison. He's assistant district attorney." After waiting while the two men shook hands, the sheriff extended the folded paper and said, "This here's a warrant for your arrest. Read it."

Hobe didn't attempt to accept the warrant; instead said, "No, you tell me."

Harbison said, "The charge is that a member of your gang — not you — attempted the murder of two LS hands last night at a boarding house in town."

"What gang and what member?" Hobe asked dryly.

"You'd know that better than we do," Harbison said. "Want me to spell it out for you?"

"You'd better."

"All right, your gang killed five LS hands

129

and put four in the hospital. Fair enough, because they attacked you while trespassing. You vandalized LS property in retaliation. Fair enough again. But when you send a man to gun down two LS hands in town, that's totally different. That's neither your range nor theirs."

"Who said I sent anyone?"

Harbison shook his head. "You boss your gang, give orders. It's hard to believe one of your gang would try it on his own. Read the warrant. You're charged with ordering and planning two murders. It doesn't matter that it didn't succeed. The intent is what counts."

"Can you prove that?"

"I'm going to try. That's why you're under arrest, with me as a witness to your arrest and to explain the reason for it."

Hobe was silent, wondering how he could handle this. Bates was inside, undoubtedly listening. Hobe didn't know exactly where the rest of the crew was, just they were out making trouble for LS, but not that kind of trouble.

Hobe looked at the sheriff. "At this boarding house, who let him in, showed him his room?"

The sheriff told him. That would be Anna.

"She recognize him?"

"Never seen him before, she said."

"She's seen every man on my crew. She doesn't know their names, but she's seen them. So, you're after the wrong man."

The sheriff said, "You could have brung him from outside, which you damn well did. Who else but you wants LS wiped out?"

"You do, for one," Hobe said.

The shock, the embarrassment, the outrage and the truth turned the sheriff's hound's face livid.

"Saddle up and come with us," the sheriff ordered.

"So you can lock me up and lose the key. Just on suspicion, with no proof? Try again, sheriff."

Harbison said, "You won't be locked up. You'll be freed under a peace bond."

"How high?"

Harbison looked around him. "What's your place worth?"

"I can show you what I paid for it." Hobe went into the bunkhouse and returned almost immediately with Parry's deed, which he extended to Harbison. The lawyer read, grunted in disgust, started to hand it back, then pocketed it.

"Look, Carew, you're missing the point — on purpose, I suspect. A peace bond means you and your crew keep the peace or lose your bond and go to jail. You're getting a favor and don't know it. The bond should be high enough that it will hurt you to forfeit it, so you control your gang instead of letting them shoot up the town and other people's property."

"You're keeping my title?"

"The court will hold it for security once the judge sets the bond."

Hobe felt an almost sick anger. And helpless. What he had planned when he could go back to his own place free of harassment from LS was to return the title to this place to Parry. If the court held the original title that would be impossible. His arrest was a blundering mistake, probably illegal, but a peace bond would free him. If he fought it he would stay in jail until the county dug up enough evidence to try him, which would be never.

"Let me leave word for the crew," he said bitterly.

When Hobe was out of earshot, Inglish said glumly, "Seely ain't goin' to like this peace-bond business."

"That's the best he can get. No identification of the gunman so no provable tie-in with Carew. Even the hurt men didn't recognize him. We lock Carew up and he'll sue the county for every dollar they've got, and win. This peace bond, if we get it, will call off his dogs."

"Not like the old days," the sheriff said sourly.

"No. Back then he'd be lynched."

In the Two Rivers Courthouse judge's chambers Hobe's bond was set at five hundred dollars, his title accepted as security.

By the time Hobe finished his supper in a

132

cafe it was dark and safe to go to Stacey's. He left his horse at the feed stable and afoot found the alley behind her place. He supposed the precaution was almost unnecessary now, but there was still one LS hand up and about who might recognize him.

Both women were in the kitchen when he knocked on the back door. It was natural to kiss them both, not only because he loved them both and they were utterly loyal to him, but because of the troubles they had been through on account of him. When he told them he'd had supper he agreed to have another cup of coffee with them.

Seated at the kitchen table, he observed them as they brought the cups and poured the coffee. Both looked tired and under strain, and when they were seated he said so.

"Why shouldn't we be? We're running a boarding house, a hospital and a shooting gallery," Stacey said with a weary smile.

"Tell me about the shooting gallery."

Stacey gestured to Anna, who only told him what he already knew, ending with, "I wish Jim would hurry back. He might know from my description of him. Why'd you send him to your old place?"

"His idea. He's curious if anything is still standing."

Stacey said, "The sheriff left here convinced one of your crew did the shooting. Has he talked to you?"

Hobe described what had happened that morning and his session with the judge in the afternoon. He summed up by saying, "What it comes down to is this. If any unidentified rider takes a shot at an LS hand here in town, I'll be blamed. I forfeit bond and I go to jail."

"To get their bond they'd have to sell your place," Anna said.

Hobe nodded. "What did this gunman look like, Anna?"

Anna described him, adding, "I didn't even get a look at his horse. Mrs. Bedloe was yelling for help and we rushed up there."

Stacey said, "One might die, Dr. Schultz says. If he does what happens to you, Hobe?"

"Jail, I reckon. Bond forfeited."

"A trial?" Stacey persisted.

"Not unless they catch the killer and he implicates me. He can't, for sure."

There came a soft knock on the back door and before anyone could rise the door opened and Jim stepped into the kitchen. He came over to the table, kissed Anna, patted Stacey's shoulder, sat down, then observed, "This looks like a council of war."

"That's just what it is," Anna said.

"Me first," Jim said. "It'll be short and not so sweet, Hobe. Your place is burned to the ground and your fence is down. All of it." He looked at Anna. "Your turn."

Anna told him what she had told Hobe, then said, "You take it from there, Hobe."

Hobe repeated what he had said to the women. When he was finished Jim was silent for a moment, then observed wryly, "We don't have a hell of a lot to celebrate, do we?" He looked at Anna. "Between us, we know everybody in this county, but you say you never saw this hardcase before."

"Maybe he doesn't live in this county," Anna said.

"Then how could he know to look right here?" Jim persisted.

Hobe said wearily, "Saloon talk. Everybody knows the hurt men were taken here."

"Not good enough. Not everybody knows there isn't a man around the place. We're too new. But this hardcase knew he had only women without guns to buck. How'd he know that?"

Jim was right, Hobe thought, coming alert. He said, "The sheriff knew it, so did his deputy. Doc knew it. Whoever delivered the grub knew it. What LS hands that dropped by to visit knew it. The neighbors, too. Who else?"

Stacey said, "Lew Seely."

Hobe and Jim looked at each other for silent seconds, both frowning in thought. Hobe broke the silence. "I can't think any owner would hire a man to gun down two of his own men, not even Seely."

Jim said, "It's got him what he wants, hasn't it? And what he wants most is you in deep, deep trouble, which you damn well are."

135

Hobe rose and, hands rammed in hip pockets, head down, began to slowly circle the kitchen. The others were silent, watching him. What Jim had just said made a savage and cruel sense, but was almost beyond comprehension. He halted and looked at Jim. "You think he'd really hire a man to do that?"

"I think he already has," Jim said. "He doesn't know our bunch. The sheriff might suspect a couple because he don't see 'em in town, but there's no proof. It's easier to bring in a stranger and claim he's one of our people." He hesitated, then asked, "Don't you see how this is shapin' up, Hobe?"

"Tell me."

"Seely brings this same man back. He hangs around town until he spots an LS hand in town. He takes a shot at him and runs. Guess who Inglish'll be after?"

"Me," Hobe said.

"Then get on the run. Head for the mountains. Let us take care of things down here." He looked at Stacey. "Why don't you go with him, Stacey? You look peaked as hell after all this business."

"No," Hobe said promptly. "Here, she'll be safe with you watchdogging things, Jim. If that hand upstairs dies I'll have the whole wolfpack after me. I want to put as much room as I can between Stacey and me. Make sense?"

"The only sense. I wasn't thinkin'."

Stacey gave Hobe a look that he interpreted as a reproving one.

After telling Anna that he'd had supper, Jim talked for a while about Hobe's place and the condition of Hobe's cattle, and his talk was interrupted by a series of jaw-cracking yawns. After the last one he came to his feet and said, "I'm gettin' old. Forty miles a day is just too damned much. I'm for bed."

Stacey said, "You go too, Anna. See you in the morning."

When they had said good night and left for Anna's room, Hobe moved over to the chair next to Stacey. Sitting down, he said, "I caught that look. You wanted to go with me."

"Yes. I want to be with you when trouble comes, like you were with me when mine came."

Hobe reached over and covered her hand with his. "I want to marry a live woman, not mourn a dead one." He rose, pulled her to her feet, put his arms around her and they kissed with a shared passion. Afterwards, with her head tucked against his chest, Stacey said, "If that's the way we both feel, let's get married tomorrow."

Hobe eased her gently back into her chair and sat down facing her, holding both her hands.

"You just aren't thinking, Stacey."

"I seldom do, but if it's going to happen

sooner or later, why not sooner?"

"That's the real weapon against me that Seely needs. How'd you like to get run down by a runaway team? Or get slugged while you're bringing in the wash, get doused with coal oil and set afire? How'd you like to have three men break in here some night and take turns raping you? Or —"

"Hobe, stop it! I see what you mean."

"Right now, I think Seely likes you and admires you," Hobe went on. "He hasn't connected us. Let's keep it that way until this is over."

Stacey sighed. "When will that be, Hobe?"

"I wish I knew," Hobe answered glumly. "All I know is we've got to keep leaning on him, starting again tomorrow."

18

Hobe felt the touch on his shoulder and woke immediately. The turned-down kitchen lamp threw just enough light into the corner for him to make out Stacey, her hair down and dressing gown belted, kneeling beside him.

"Hobe, are you awake?" she asked in a low voice.

Hobe raised himself on his elbows. "Anything wrong?"

"Mrs. Bedloe just woke me. The man upstairs died."

"She's sure."

"She's a nurse. She should know." She rose, saying, "Get your pants on. I'll get breakfast."

Hobe looked out the window behind him. False dawn was beginning. Stacey was stirring up the banked coal fire in the stove. Hobe dressed, went over to the stove, turned Stacey around and kissed her. He said then, "That's got to last you awhile. Don't make breakfast for me. Just some bread and coffee and I'm off."

"To where, Hobe?"

"Anywhere but here."

·While Hobe ate his bread and drank his coffee Stacey made a stack of beef sandwiches. As he ate he gave her instructions to pass on to Jim. There was a stage relay station in the foothills north of town. After Jim found what the sheriff planned to do about the death of the LS hand Hobe would meet him in mid-afternoon at the station after he picked up some powder and fuses.

Afterwards, he made up his blanketroll, sandwiches inside, strapped on his gun and shellbelt and faced Stacey, who was watching him.

"Why the powder and fuse, Hobe?"

"I'm going to raise some hell with it."

"There'll be a reward out for you, Hobe. That means anybody can kill you for money."

"And if anybody tries I can kill him," Hobe replied. He shouldered his blanketroll, said, "You take care and so will I." He didn't kiss her again, it would seem to her too much like a permanent good-bye.

It was almost daylight when he reached the stable. There he found the hostler forking down hay from the loft to the horses gathered in the corral below. Hobe found his saddle astride a stall partition, caught his dun, saddled up and, because he had paid the man last night, only waved to the hostler in parting.

The town was coming awake as he rode through it. Smoke from breakfast fires was lofting into the dawn sky but there was almost nothing moving on the streets. Crossing the south bridge, he picked up the road that would take him to LS.

He wondered what the day would hold for Stacey. Early, maybe even now, Mrs. Bedloe would be on her way to tell Dr. Schultz he had lost a patient during the night. The doctor would head for the hardware store as soon as it was open to tell the undertaker to pick up the body. Word would soon reach Sheriff Inglish. Either he would come to Stacey's (unlikely) or Jim would prowl the saloons and maybe the courthouse to learn if there was a warrant out for Hobe's arrest.

Would the sheriff send a messenger to LS to tell Seely his man had died? Again unlikely, since the machinery was already in motion against Hobe. Besides, Seely would be in town shortly and learn of the death.

Hobe left the road for a low ridge of piñon-stippled hills. From there he could see the road while the piñons screened him. He rode slowly so his horse wouldn't raise dust. A pair of riders passed below him and never looked up.

When the buggy came in sight, headed for town, he cut down a draw deep enough to hide him and his horse and waited behind a pair of screening piñons close to the road.

As the buggy drew close he moved his dun between the trees and onto the road. As he had hoped, it was Lew Seely on his way to the bank, and this time he was alone.

At sight of Hobe barring his way, Seely reined in his horse and the two men looked at each other.

"Turned road agent, have you?" Seely said.

Hobe shook his head. "Bankers never carry money. It's too precious to lose."

Seely's face looked gray and somehow ravaged. He said sharply then, "What is it you want? Why've you stopped me?"

"To talk."

"You know where I do business. See me there. Now get out of my way."

Hobe gestured to a tall cedar tree across the road. "Let's move over to some shade."

"I'm in some shade. If you want to talk, come to the bank. There's shade there, too. Now move."

For answer, Hobe moved his horse up to Seely's, reached out, grasped the horse's bridle and spurred his own dun. Surprisingly, Seely's horse allowed himself to be led off the road into the shade of the cedar. Hobe let go of the bridle, dismounted, ground-haltered his dun, moved over to the cedar, sat down and put his back against its trunk.

Seely's face had colored with anger. He made no move to step down and join Hobe.

"Can you hear me from there?" Hobe asked quietly.

"I hear you."

"About that peace bond you laid on me. Tell Harbison you've changed your mind. Have him ask the judge to lift it."

"Why should I? What's changed? Not you. Not your hoodlums."

"Let's see," Hobe began thoughtfully. "You own and lease out that saloon and settler's store on the far edge of Fort Monroe. You own and lease out a sawmill in the Dexters. Then there's that big warehouse on the riverfront. You also own a good silver-lead mine and mill up in the Dexters. You —"

"Of course I own them, and more too! What are you trying to do — threaten me?"

"Why do you think I've been talking? I purely am threatening you."

"You fool! I'll have you in jail before the week's out, and you'll stay there for a long, long time."

"You still aren't really listening, are you? First, your only love is money and property, so that's your soft spot. That's how I can hurt you."

"Remember Harbison's deal?" Seely asked dryly. "We keep this fight on our own ranges or we're in trouble. If you plan harm to the properties you named they aren't on my range. If you move against them you'll be hunted down and locked up."

"What if both or one of your men shot in that boarding house dies?"

"The same thing, only you'll be charged with being an accessory to murder. You're the boss of the man who shot them on your orders."

Hobe smiled faintly. "You'll have some trouble proving that. Now let's go back to these properties of yours I named. Your others, too. Are they all insured?"

Seely said coldly, "That's no business of yours, but I assure you they are."

Hobe plucked a piece of grass, nibbled on it, then tossed it aside. "Funny thing about these insurance companies. Say a man with lots of property like you has a bad fire. The company pays off. Then he has another fire on another property. Then a third fire and explosion, maybe a fourth. These companies get together with each other. They agree so-and-so is a bad risk. Maybe he's setting the fires himself to collect a lot of money. The insurance companies cancel his policies. He can't get insurance from any company because the word has got around. Is that true?"

Seely said in a voice thickened with anger, "It's true! It's also blackmail!"

"Have I asked you for any money?" Hobe asked innocently.

"Indirectly. And you'll not get a penny from me by your threats. I can protect my property."

"But you can't. You're shorthanded now. You can't even spare a man to drive you. You can't spread a dozen men in twenty places, even if you still have the dozen."

"If you damage any of my outside property I'll have a U.S. Marshal in here to pick you up. That's a promise."

In a neighboring tree a pair of piñon jays started to quarrel noisily.

Hobe said above their chatter, "Good. While he's here I'll show him my Silver Creek homestead you flattened."

"I'll list your threats, believe me!" Seely said coldly.

"Why, Mr. Seely, we've never even talked to each other except out at the Parry place. We had a witness then, the sheriff." He gestured toward the near tree. "Two jays and two horses heard this. I don't think they'll talk in court, so you have nobody to verify we talked at all. So no talk took place, as far as I'll remember. You'll have to prove it did, and you can't."

Seely gave a look of purest hatred but Hobe went on without letting up. "Some piece of your property will be burned down or blown up tonight. You don't know where and it's too late to stop it even if you did. That'll be the first one until you go to the judge."

"I can't tell a judge to reverse a ruling!" Seely said angrily.

"Why not? You paid for his election." Hobe rose and said, "That's all, so drive on. Somebody might need some money."

Hobe watched him furiously whip his horse back onto the road, headed for town.

"When that hearse pulls down the street the whole town knows somebody died. In town, not outside it," Jim said. "The kids follow it, then run back and tell everybody where it stopped."

He and Hobe were squatted in a cottonwood motte well off the stage road below the relay station, their horses hidden in the thicket. Jim had arrived first, found the cottonwoods, then watched the road and whistled Hobe down.

"Did the sheriff show up at Stacey's?"

Jim shook his head. "He didn't have to. The first saloon I hit, the fat deputy had hit first, tryin' to raise a posse. Like the kids say in tag game, 'You're it.' "

Hobe nodded and then told Jim of his interception of Seely, his threats and Seely's counterthreats. "He left some worried and plenty

145

mad. Of course, when he hits town and finds out about the dead man he'll be happy."

"And hungry to get you. What do I do?"

"First — as you love Anna — stay the hell away from me. Later, we'll talk about where you can leave grub for me. Right now, here's what I need to know. What does he own that I can burn or blow up without hurting anybody that works for him? Tonight, because I promised him."

Jim frowned and was lost in thought for moments. Finally he said, "Well, at headquarters they got a pretty big blacksmith and tool shop over that ridge west of the bunkhouse. Seely put it there because he didn't like the racket close to the house."

"Anybody sleep there?"

"No. It's walkin' distance from the bunkhouse even for a crippled cowpoke."

Hobe smiled and shook his head. "Just right. What I promised, the day I promised it."

"He may have a lookout there, Hobe."

"I'm gambling he won't. He's expecting the trouble will happen off his range. Besides, he's shorthanded and what's left of his crew is overworked. He tells one of his hands to stand lookout all night and he's lost him." He paused for a moment. "How does this sound? I take off now, get to LS before dark, and watch the blacksmith shop through glasses. If I see the men leave for the bunkhouse and nobody comes to the shop, I wait until dark. If no lamp is lit in the shop at dark, I assume it's empty."

"Sounds all right, but make a little racket before you go inside. Anybody in there would call out to identify yourself. He wouldn't want to shoot a friend."

Hobe nodded and they both rose and went into the thicket to their horses. Hobe decided that this was as good a place as any to make camp, and tossed his blanketroll in the bush beside a small stream that meandered through the thicket. Jim tossed a couple of small sacks of oats on top of Hobe's blanket-roll, then transferred his saddlebags, holding the black powder and fuse cord to Hobe's dun. They agreed to meet there in two days. With a little time, Jim could come up with some more targets.

As Hobe was leading his dun out of the thicket, Jim alongside him said, "There's plenty of fuse cord so use a lot of it tonight. I got an Indian hunch that tool shed is likely the powder house too, so get good and clear of it."

As Hobe was tightening his cinch Jim said, "I'm headin' for Parry's place. The sheriff'll be out with a pack of saloon bums, likely tomorrow. If any of the boys are back do I tell 'em to scatter?"

"Tell 'em to go home and say nothing. We'll be in touch." Then he added, "When the sheriff comes, don't be wearing a gun, Jim. Half of them will be trigger happy and packing bottles. Just a warm-up for the Fourth of July."

"Damn! I'd forgotten it's so close. Three — four days?"

"Four."

"All right. I'll be a dumb Indian." He grinned and waved Hobe on, saying, "Have a happy blow-up. . . ."

Hobe crowded his dun a little bit, but he was halted in the thin foothill timber above LS when he heard the clang of the iron calling all hands to supper. Taking up his glasses, he focused on the blacksmith shop, a large affair of weather-worn logs and clapboard, a small and empty holding corral on the side of it.

Presently, two men came from the shop into view and climbed the road to the ridge and disappeared behind it. Hobe sat down, his back against a tree trunk, and glassed the ridge from time to time. If anyone showed, it would be after supper and close to dark, he reckoned.

Afterwards, he checked the sacked powder bags and added more cord to that already wrapped around the powder. All the while he kept an eye on the ridge. Nobody crossed over it. The setting sun was behind the Dexters, throwing the valley below in deep shadow that was darkening by the minute.

When it was so dark he could barely make out the building, he swung into the saddle and headed for it. With the swiftness of a mountain sundown, almost-total darkness was around him when he reached the building. He circled it, saw that the double doors of the shop were propped open and the shop lightless.

Tethering his dun at the corral, he unpacked the powder, then took out the extra fuse cord. After tying the end of the cord wrapped around the powder to the saddle horn, he moved slowly toward the open double doors, unwinding the cord as he walked. Two or three times on his way he paused to hammer his fist against the clapboard siding. No reaction came from inside the building.

His eyes accustomed to the dark, he slowly moved into the interior of the shop, trailing the cord. The fire in the forge glowed dimly, almost out, its day's work over. By its faint light Hobe found the partition separating the shop from the tool shed. He stripped off the remaining cord and placed the powder between the forge and the partition. Afterwards, he backtracked to his dun, with the cord as his guideline. There, he joined part of his extra cord to the charge cord and walked his dun slowly north, cord in one hand, reins in the other, until he felt the cord tauten.

He halted, looked back and could see no building. If he lighted the fuse and stayed there, was he out of harm's way? He wanted to wait there and watch, but he remembered Jim's admonition to clear out quick, just in case the tool shed was also a powder storage. Jim's 'Indian hunches' were mostly right.

Kneeling, Hobe struck a match and held it below the fuse cord. In two seconds it flared and sputtered and the sparks were on their way. He mounted reluctantly and put his dun at a canter, looking back over his shoulder. Sometimes he could see the powder sparks, sometimes not, depending on the terrain. Finally, he could see no sparks and he wondered if the connection he'd made had somehow failed.

And then came a thunderous explosion and a brilliant flash of light through the double doors. Before its echo had died there was a bigger, ground-shaking blast that momentarily lighted up the night. He could see sections of the roof cartwheeling into the sky, some afire. The building itself was beginning to blaze.

As Hobe urged his dun on into the darkness ahead, he could hear the sky-borne debris hit the ground behind him.

19

Lew Seely stood apart from the LS crew on the ridge, watching the bonfire of the blacksmith shop grow larger, shooting sparks into the night sky.

Dana Keyhoe drifted over and halted beside him. "How the hell could he know we stored our powder there?" the foreman growled.

The question wasn't worth answering any more than the fire was worth fighting. Seely turned and went down the ridge, crossed the creek, entered his lamplit office and sat down in the chair behind the desk.

What a hell of a day this had been. But still, in spite of the fire over the hill, it held a promise of eventual victory. He had reached town still in a wrathful mood after his meeting with Carew, and tied his horse and rig in the side alley of the bank. He'd said good morning to the two clerks and was scarcely seated at his desk when Jessup knocked on the side door and was allowed to enter.

After closing the door behind him, Jessup had come over to the desk and said, "Excuse me, sir, but the sheriff was in to see you earlier. He just left."

"Did he say why he wanted to see me?"

"Yes, sir. One of your men at the boarding house died in the night. He's raising a posse to hunt the killer."

"I'll see him." Jessup had left, and Seely had put aside the morning statement on his desk to consider this news. Had Carew known that the man had died? No, how could he? If he'd known of it would he have made his threats? No, he would have run and hid.

Then Seely had done some careful thinking.

As Carew had pointed out, he was short-handed and vulnerable wherever he had money invested. Much as he had hated the thought, he had known what he had to do — ask the judge to withdraw the peace-bond ruling on Carew.

Less than an hour later he, Harbison and Sheriff Inglish had met with County Judge Joe Enden in his office just off the courtroom at the courthouse. Enden was a white-haired party hack who relied entirely on Harbison for advice.

When they had been seated he had stated his request that Carew's peace bond be voided, or, in his words, "Whatever it takes to cancel it."

"But he's responsible for this man's death," Harbison had protested.

"You can't prove that or he'd be in jail now, with a trial date set," Seely had replied. "He wasn't the man who fired the gun and you don't know who did."

Inglish had said in reply, "You're the one that thought of the peace bond, Lew."

"And I'm sorry I did." He had gone on to tell of his conversation a couple of hours earlier with Carew. He had finished by saying, "I want the peace bond lifted." To the sheriff he said, "Cancel that posse, Burt. Get the word around fast that Carew is not wanted — repeat *not*. Anybody who braces him is subject to arrest." He had leaned forward in his chair.

"I'm telling the simple truth. I haven't got the men and neither has the county to night-and-day guard my holdings." Then he had risen. "Burt, as soon as your deputy has called off the posse, send him out to the east line camp. Bates Jordan will be there. Have him tell Bates that Carew is free as a bird."

Seely rose. The smoke from the fire could be smelled in the room, despite the fact that new glass had replaced the broken pane. At the liquor cabinet Seely poured himself a short drink of whiskey and went back to his chair.

Obviously, Carew hadn't gotten the word that his peace bond had been lifted. Still, he might have and ignored it, since the blacksmith shop was on LS range and fair game. As fires went, it was a trivial one, but nevertheless, it was a warning. Carew had promised he would make trouble today and he had kept his word.

And then what had been in the back of his mind since his morning meeting with the judge and sheriff began to take shape. Naturally, he wanted Carew freed of his peace bond if only to preserve his own property. But why had he emphasized to the sheriff that Carew be told he had the run of the town and was free as a bird?

Because, Seely thought now, he'd wanted Carew within reach, pinpointed and accessible. It hadn't occurred to him this morning, but it did now. Fourth of July was only a few days away. On the Fourth the whole county population came into Two Rivers. There would be gunfire, powder blasts and firecrackers from dawn till dark, along with horse races, tugs of war, drinking, fist, knife and gunfights and saloon brawls. What better cover for an accidental shooting?

20

Hobe took the whole morning and into the afternoon to make his way to the Parry place. He kept to what cover was available, watched his backtrail and waited patiently to pick up any sign of the posse. When he reached Juniper Creek he still found no signs that a large group of riders had passed headed south, and he was puzzled. Had the sheriff told the posse to ride out singly and stake out the Parry place and wait? That was possible, but unlikely, since Inglish wasn't that clever.

Hobe crossed the creek and traveled up it, the thick alders screening him from the faint road he normally traveled. When he was close to the place he put his dun up a rise and glassed it. It seemed abandoned, but Jim's favorite black was in the corral. He glassed the surrounding country and saw a few cattle grazing, which they wouldn't be doing if there were men or horses around.

It looked safe, almost too safe.

Hobe crossed the creek and was approaching the corral when he heard the rhythmic chopping of an ax coming from the barn, which served as their woodshed. He rode up to the open door and Jim, hearing his horse approach, was in the doorway, ax in hand, when he reined up.

"How'd it go?" Jim asked.

"Biggest bonfire I ever watched," Hobe said. "You were right about the powder in the tool shed. If you'd listened close you could have heard it here." He looked at the house and bunkhouse and nothing was changed. "Anything happened here, like a posse?"

"Turn out your horse. Nothing's happened here and nothing will. Bates'll tell you." Then he laughed at the blank surprise showing on Hobe's face.

As Hobe led his horse into the corral and unsaddled, he was thinking of Jim's last words. Jim was waiting for him halfway to the bunkhouse, a load of cut wood in his arms; together they headed for the kitchen.

Inside, the kitchen was empty. Jim dumped his wood in the woodbox by the cold stove and then led the way through the cookshack, waited by the far door and waved Hobe ahead of him, then closed the door behind him. Both bunkhouse doors were open and the room was abuzz with flies. "Seely cornered all the window glass and screen wire in town, so we sleep in Parry's house," Jim said.

They went out the creekside door and found Bates Jordan sitting in a barrel chair in the shade of the building, peeling potatoes.

"Well, here's the boss man back," Bates said and grinned his broad, near-toothless smile. "Jim tell you I had a caller today?"

"The sheriff?"

"Hell, he won't ride unless somebody makes him," Bates said. "It was that fat deputy of his. He wanted you and I told him I didn't know where or how to find you, so he left word. You ain't wanted by the law on account of that fellow died. The posse's been called off. Your peace bond is clean lifted. The deed's in the cookshack. As long as you and Seely hack at each other on your own ranges it's all right. But if you do any damage to Seely's 'outside holdings' you'll be arrested. What's an 'outside holding'?"

"Anything that's not on LS range," Hobe said. He looked at Jim. "How do you read it?"

Jim said, "I think you got Seely between a rock and a hard place."

"What about last night? That might change Seely's mind," Hobe said. "And he can change the mind of everybody in that courthouse."

"Don't think he'll try. That blacksmith shop was nothin' compared to what you could do to him, and he knows it."

"What blacksmith shop?" Bates asked.

When Hobe described the blowing up of the

shop and the stored powder, Bates smiled and said, "I wished I'd been there."

Afterwards, Hobe was silent, thinking over Bates' news. Somehow, in a way he couldn't explain to himself, this had been too easy. Yesterday, as he'd ridden out to intercept Seely, he had anticipated Seely's iron refusal to take seriously the threats he would make. He had also judged that once Seely reached town and learned one of his crew had died, he would post a dead-or-alive reward for Hobe's capture. Weeks, even months, of being on the dodge had seemed a certainty.

And now this. No posse, no reward out, peace bond lifted and deed returned; no warrant for his arrest. This wasn't the old Seely he knew, and now he came to his decision.

"Jim, I'm heading for town."

"Wrong day, Hobe. They'll be buryin' that LS hand today."

"Maybe in town, but more likely at the ranch. Anyway, I want to know if I'm free or if I'm walking into a prize sucker's trap. I've got to find out sometime."

Jim looked thoughtful and then nodded briefly. "Yeah, one man on a roof with a rifle. If he's caught he says he heard there was a posse after you. He gets paid by Seely afterwards." He rose and nodded. "Let's make it tomorrow."

"Who invited you?"

"I did. I got eyes in the back of my head and

I don't see any in the back of yours."

"And why tomorrow? Why not now?"

Jim sighed. "Look, I stopped by the hardware store last night. The funeral is in the town cemetery this afternoon. The LS crew hasn't had a day off since we blew the dam. They'll go to the funeral or quit, and Seely knows it. They'll be drunk at the funeral and drunker afterwards. And who killed the friend they just buried? Nobody but —"

"Hobe Carew," Hobe said. "So today we'd be walking into a ready-made gunfight."

"Against those odds, who the hell wants one," Jim said.

Late next morning Hobe and Jim rode up to the courthouse tie rail together, but only Hobe dismounted.

"See you at the Cameo," Jim said and rode off.

Hobe entered the courthouse and headed straight for the sheriff's office. Inglish was alone in the big room, standing by a side window. When he saw Hobe he came back to his desk and waved him to the deputy's chair.

When Hobe was seated Inglish said in a mild tone of voice, "Come in to check out Ed's story, didn't you?" At Hobe's nod, the sheriff said, "Well, if he told you what I said to tell you, you're a free man. The peace bond lifted, no charges, no posse and no reward out."

"But what changed Seely's mind that fast?"

"I reckon his talk with you yesterday. It worried the hell out of him."

"It was meant to."

"I wish him and you would quit this janglin'. It don't make any sense wreckin' each other's places like a couple of damn kids."

"Who wanted the peace bond? I didn't," Hobe countered. "Who wrecked two of my places? I didn't."

"Well, he's willin' to quit. Don't liftin' that peace bond tell you that?"

"Did he say so?"

"Yesterday. Said he'd made a mistake and was sorry he'd done it."

"If he'll quit, so will I," Hobe said.

The sheriff pondered for a moment, then said, "Tell you what. You'll be goin' to the Fourth of July races, won't you?"

"I reckon so, why?"

"Well, Lew Seely is the finish-line judge. His bank gives the prize. Why not look him up out there and tell him what you just told me — you'll quit if he quits. Shake hands with him and be seen with him."

"For any particular reason?"

"A damned good one. There'll be a lot of drinkin' out there. Some of those boys might forget the posse was called off and that you're not wanted. But if they see you talkin' friendly with Seely and ask around, they'll know you're not wanted. He'll be your protection."

"Will Seely like this any more than I do?"

"Why not?" the sheriff asked. "He'll be makin' up for a lot of his pigheaded notions. At any rate, I'll know in short order. Where'll you be?"

"The Cameo."

"That's an LS hangout."

"And that's why I'm going. The sooner I show them I'm a big boy now, the sooner they'll believe it."

Hobe joined Jim, who was bellied up to the bend of the long bar at the Cameo. Neither the bar nor the gambling tables were really crowded, but a lot of men were there at this usually slow hour, and they were drinking it up, too.

Hobe ordered a beer and got a careful look from the bartender before he went back to draw the beer. On his way he picked up a couple of empties and spoke casually to a couple of drinkers.

"What did the good sheriff say?" Jim asked.

"It's all true, I'm free as a bird."

"Free as a sittin' duck," Jim corrected softly. "Did you watch that bartender? He's got you marked and already got the word out. Drink your beer fast and let's get the hell out of here."

Hobe shook his head in negation. "Nope. If I can't go anywhere alone in this town and take care of myself, I'd better start wearing didies and a bib."

"I was afraid of that, but if you think that's

chasin' me off, you're crazy." He waited for the bartender to bring Hobe's beer, then ordered another for himself.

While they were waiting for Jim's beer Hobe told of the sheriff's notion that Hobe join Seely at the races, shake hands with him and be seen with him in order to establish to anyone watching that the two men had settled their differences and that Hobe was not wanted by the law.

"Do it," Jim said. He thought for a moment, then said, "You haven't been here long enough to be known to a lot of people. But everybody's heard of your scrap with LS. Once they get the word you're friendly with Seely they'll forget the bounty huntin'." His beer came and he took a sip of it, then said, "I didn't think Inglish was that smart. Seely's said yes to it, I reckon?"

"The sheriff is with him now. He'll stop by here with the word."

A big puncher down the bar finished, put down his glass, slapped his companion on the shoulder, then turned and headed for the swinging doors. He walked past without looking at them.

Then a deep, slurred voice said from behind them, "Turn around, Carew!"

Both Hobe and Jim turned and saw the gun in the big puncher's fist. As any prudent man would, Jim slowly lifted his hands shoulder high and took two steps sideways, silently proclaiming he wasn't a party to this trouble.

"Lift your gun with your left hand and drop it on the floor."

"Why should I?" Hobe asked.

"Because I'm takin' you to the courthouse and turnin' you over to the sheriff."

"I just left the sheriff," Hobe said firmly, so every man in the room could hear him. "If he wanted me, why am I here?"

"You're lyin'!"

"He'll be right here in a few minutes. Ask him if I am." Hobe turned his back on the puncher and picked up his beer.

For three stunned seconds the puncher stood, unbelieving, and then he started to lift his gun from hip to eye level.

Quick as thought, Jim moved toward the puncher, at the same time lifting out his own gun. He smashed his left shoulder into the bigger man, knocking him off balance. With gun in right hand, he slashed down savagely at the wrist of the puncher's gun hand, and saw and heard the gun drop out of it onto the floor.

Hobe wheeled at the sound of the scuffle. When he saw what was happening, he lifted out his own gun, placed it on the bartop and moved toward the big puncher. The roomful of men watched silently as Hobe reached the puncher, who was bent over holding his wrist. Without hesitation Hobe cuffed off the puncher's Stetson, grabbed a handful of hair

162

and pulled the puncher's head down, at the same time lifting a knee into the big man's face.

·The puncher shouted with pain, reared back, lost his balance, staggered sideways and crashed into the wall. Already his nose was gushing blood over his lips. Hobe kicked the dropped gun under the gambling table and stood hands on hips, waiting.

But not for long. The puncher came up in a swift, low charge that Hobe tripped before the man had balance. The puncher fell, rolled like a cat, and was on his feet instantly, facing Hobe.

By separate decision both men charged and collided. Hobe pushed back by more weight. From then on it was pure barroom brawl. The puncher fought as if he'd never lost a fight and never intended to. Hobe took punishment until he realized every roundhouse swing was predictable and telegraphed, and left the puncher's midriff open. Hobe moved inside the wild, swinging arms and sank a right into the belly. He discovered the puncher was not only big but fat and soft-bellied. It took just three driving blows to bring the big man's arms down to protect his belly, and then Hobe threw a looping left to the jaw, which swiveled the puncher's head. His arms dropped, he fell to his knees, then pitched on his face.

Hobe was reaching for his gun on the bartop when the batwings were pushed open and

Sheriff Inglish stepped into the saloon, and halted abruptly. He glanced at the downed man, then at Hobe, and lastly at the men who had gathered in a tight group to watch the fight.

"What happened?" the sheriff asked.

"A bounty hunter, I reckon," Hobe said, and told of his refusal to be taken to the court-house under the puncher's gun.

"That like it happened?" the sheriff asked the crowd. Some men nodded, others shrugged, a few said they only watched the fist fight.

"All right. Listen to me, every man-Jack of you. This man is *not* wanted by me or any other law officer. There are *no* charges against him. There is *no* reward for his delivery to me. Anyone that brings him in will get arrested." He paused, then added, "Spread the word around." He pointed to the unconscious puncher. "Tell it to that rock-head when he wakes up."

He skirted the puncher on the floor, came up beside Hobe and said, "Seely agrees on the Fourth meeting. He still says he's sorry it happened."

21

A distant but careful look at the man repairing Musick's horse-pasture fence told Seely this was not Will Musick, but his one-man crew. He rode on in the blazing heat to the sorry shack and saw Musick standing in its doorway, as if expecting him.

As Seely dismounted under the cottonwood and tied his horse beside Musick's, he heard footsteps approaching.

"Hot day, Mr. Seely."

Seely turned, took off his hat and wiped his face and forehead. "I can prove that. How've you been, Will?"

"Like always." He gestured toward the barn. "That place of mine's an oven. I reckon the barn would be cooler."

Together they headed for the open barn doors, Musick's sweat-wet shirt clinging to his massive chest. Seely felt hot but he appeared his cool, immaculate self. Inside the barn there was a wagon pushed far back. On the dirt behind its tailgate were two ancient easy chairs, the stuffing leaking from the seats and backs. Seely guessed they had been moved from the cabin so both men could escape the heat.

Musick waited until Seely had chosen his chair and sat down, then seated himself and said, "You're lookin' tired, Mr. Seely. Been workin' too hard?"

"That, among other things. Like riding into town yesterday to bury one of the men you shot in the boarding house."

Musick was about to protest, thought better of it and remained silent, his dark eyes watchful.

"I've got another job for you, Will," Seely said easily.

"Like the other one? If that's it, no thanks. I'm not in that business."

"Oh, but you are, like it or not. Think a minute."

Musick did and finally said, "You'll call in my note."

"Among other things," Seely agreed. "Things like telegraphing the Cattle Association where Tom Sauers can be picked up, and what name he's using. I've still got the detective's card."

"What if I tell them you paid me to shoot two of your crew?"

Seely smiled and shook his head. "Who'd believe it? It's the word of a cattle thief against the word of a rancher and bank president."

Musick rose, scowling, moved to the doorway and rammed both hands in his hip pockets, looking at his cabin. "Is this in town, same

166

place? Because if it is, that Injun woman at the boardin' house saw me." He turned and said, "I don't like this, Seely, not any part of it. Get somebody else."

"Come back and listen to me."

Reluctantly, Musick went back to his chair and sat down, his expression both defiant and stubborn.

Seely said, "Now to begin with, this won't even be close to the boarding house. Do you think she could pick you out of two or three hundred men, even if she's there?"

"Where?"

"The Fourth of July horse races out on the flats north of town. There'll be shooting aplenty, especially at the end of a race. There'll be falling-down drunks, too. You couldn't find a safer place for it to happen."

"Out in the open? God Almighty! You're crazy!"

"Have you ever been to one of those horse races on the Fourth?"

"No."

"You have to see it to believe it," Seely went on calmly. "We draw most of the people in three counties. Steamboats come up from Riverbend, soldiers from Monroe. The race stakes are high. I know because the bank puts up the prize money. You're a horse breeder. I'm surprised you haven't entered some of your horses."

"Oh, I've heard about it, but most of my stuff

is too young or too old." Musick came back to the subject. "How do you expect me to find one man in three hundred? By description? It can't be done."

"He'll be with me and I'll be at the finish line as a judge. There will be a tent there, close. The winners come there for their prize money."

"What's this man look like?" Musick persisted.

"Taller than either of us, not so heavy as you. Dark skin, black hair, clean-shaved. He travels around with a big half-breed, but he's got gray in his hair. Don't mix up the two. Your man is about thirty, the breed's in his middle forties." Seely rose from his chair. "Do you agree, or do I write Texas?"

Musick swore under his breath. "All right," he said in a grudging voice. "Let's see your money."

Seely reached into his hip pocket, took out a roll of bank notes bound by a rubber band and tossed them in the chair beside Musick. "One-thirty on the Fourth at the race course. There will be a lot of men talking with me that afternoon. When you see me take off my hat and wipe the sweat from my forehead I'll be talking to Carew."

When Musick only nodded Seely walked over to his horse, mounted and rode off without a look behind him. Musick, still seated in his chair, counted the money, put the bills in his shirt pocket and leaned back in the chair, looking at nothing.

This was one hell of a way to earn money, he reflected, but it was better than being hanged for a horse thief or rotting away in a Texas jail. Trouble was, he could see no end to it. Seely owned him body and soul. *He'll keep on owning me until one of us dies,* he thought.

Suddenly, his eyes focused; he backtracked on his bitter reverie. *Until one of us dies* stuck in his memory. Why did it have to be him, hanged or in jail?

For appalled seconds, Musick reflected on this. He was certain Seely had told no one of his involvement in the boarding-house shootings. If he had, then Musick would have been picked up days ago. His only known connection with Seely was a routine bank loan.

Now, excitement pushing him, Musick rose and moved to the barn's doorway and looked up at the brassy sky. Would Seely have taken notes of what the Cattle Association man told him? He doubted it. What would his Board of Directors think, now or in the future, if they read he had loaned bank money to a wanted horse thief? They'd spread the story, certain enough.

That left Musick with a question he couldn't answer. Could he get away with shooting a man in the drunken turmoil at the Fourth races? Seely thought so and had put up a lot

169

of money to back his judgment, money which he dare not claim.

Thinking very carefully now, Musick decided he would play this by sight and sound. If the races went as Seely predicted they would, he could get away with it. If not, he would return Seely's money.

But, naturally enough, he wanted to keep Seely's money.

22

Dawn of the Fourth of July was ushered in by a tremendous blast of Giant powder in the foothills north of town. It was calculated to rouse all citizens to a busy day of noise, fun, parades, band music, speeches, drilling contests, both single-jack and double-jack, and, of course, the afternoon horse races.

Hobe, Bates and Jim rode in from the Parry place close to noon. Yesterday, as Bates Jordan had predicted they would, Hobe's roving crew had drifted in and reported their wrecking operations before taking off for town. It had made Hobe wonder if Seely, adding up his losses, would have a change of heart and refuse to be seen with him today.

The town streets were crowded with riders and wagons, the stretches of boardwalk filled with people. Somewhere on the far side of town a crowd cheered a winner of some contest. Bates headed for the cheers, while Hobe and Jim rode for Stacey's. Firecrackers, occasional gunshots and braying bugles were background noises in the hot noonday sun.

As usual, Hobe and Jim tied their horses in the alley. There was little chance of being noticed because of the crowds and activities in town. When they walked in the back door Stacey and Anna were dishing up their own plates. Both women got soundly kissed and hugged by their men.

After they were finished eating and the crowd in the dining room had drifted out, Hobe and Jim helped clear the dining-room tables.

The women wanted to talk, so they let the dishes go and sat down around the kitchen table.

"Well, from now on you can use the front door," Stacey said. "LS and Bedloe cleared out the day of the funeral." She looked closely at Hobe. "You've been in a fight. Your cheekbone's swelled up."

Hobe told of the Cameo brawl and of Jim saving him from a bullet. Then he told of the hoped-for truce with Seely this afternoon at the races.

"Who thought up this meeting?" Anna asked.

"The sheriff," Hobe said.

Anna looked at Jim. "You like it? Hobe and Seely friends?"

"If Hobe's seen with Seely, it could cool off things, like that Cameo business. Besides, I'll be with Hobe. Seely won't know it, but I'll be there."

Hobe looked at the kitchen clock; it was after one o'clock. "I'd kind of like to be at the first race just so I don't worry Seely."

"All right. Let's get going."

Hobe stood up, unbuckled his shellbelt and tossed it, with his gun, on the table.

As soon as it touched the tabletop Anna said sharply, "Hobe, keep it! What if you're walking into an ambush?"

"No. This is kind of a peace parley. Seely never carries a gun, so far as I know, so I won't. It's taking an advantage over him, and he'd resent it."

"He doesn't need to carry a gun! He hires them!" Anna said hotly. She looked at her husband. "Jim, make him see sense!"

Jim thought for a moment, then said, "If it's an honest-to-God ambush, his gun won't make the difference. But it's the wrong place and the wrong time for it. Too damn many witnesses to it, instead of alone in a dark alley."

"All drunk and won't remember," Anna said bitterly. She rose, walked over to Hobe and put her arms around him and kissed him. "I hope this isn't good-bye, but I'm afraid it is."

Hobe smiled down at her. "If you feel that way, Anna, I'll get dressed."

He reached down, picked up his shellbelt

and strapped it on.

He and Jim went out to their horses. When they were out of sight of the house, Hobe reined up, took off his shellbelt and handed it to Jim, who put it in his saddlebag. No words were necessary. They headed for the race course.

Will Musick immediately spotted the tent by the finish line but he didn't go to it directly. The flat was thronged with riders, wagons and buggies, and a few dozen picnic cloths were spread out beside the vehicles.

The crowd surely numbered in the hundreds, mostly men and boys, although there was a scattering of women and small children. More people afoot were crossing the bridge to swell the crowd under a clear sky and hot sun.

On the quarter mile racing track and on a strip just east of it riders were practicing starts and spurts of speed and already a faint haze of dust hung over the track. Men were already lined up beside the track, looking over the horses and making their bets. And drinking openly, for this was a man's event; if the women didn't like it they didn't have to look. There was the racket of firecrackers and random gunfire, just for the hell of it.

Musick made his easy circle of the track. Slowly, groups of people were beginning to form close to the finish line. Assessing the situation, Musick decided that Seely was right in his judgment that this milling and confusion would cover any happening.

As he rode around the ever-swelling groups that were collecting around both sides of the finish line he came to the conclusion that what he was going to do would be best done afoot. There should be no pellmell escape. Do it, then join the curious crowd.

He dismounted beside one of several empty wagons behind the tent, tied his horse to a rear wheel of the wagon, as others had done with several of the wagons, then made his way past the tent to the restless crowd beyond the finish line. Seely, with Carew, would be exactly at the freshly limed white finish stripe.

With his formidable weight Musick had no trouble making his way through the loosely formed crowd. He came to a halt when only a few men were between him and Seely. Carew, taller and more tanned than Seely, was beside him. Neither man, both in shirtsleeves, wore a gun, he noticed.

A bugle sounded a raucous off-key assembly at the far end of the course and by the slow movement of the crowd and the riders Musick judged the first race was about to begin.

He let the first race go by without watching it, instead studying the people around him. As Seely predicted, there was a lot of noise and gunfire after the finish and more open drinking. He watched Seely excuse himself from Hobe and head for the tent to pay off the winner. Around Musick, men were paying off or collecting bets. He had the pattern. He looked carefully at Hobe. So this was the Carew man Seely wanted dead at almost any cost. His Indian partner wasn't around, so far as Musick could tell.

The assembly call sounded again as Seely made his way back to Hobe's side. Then Seely took off his hat and mopped his brow with his handkerchief. That was Seely's signal that the man he was talking to was Carew.

The crowd started to move closer to the race course and Musick let himself be shoved closer to Seely.

The starting cannon boomed and the cheering and yelling started up again. Musick waited, watching Seely, whose back was to him. When the tremble of the earth underfoot announced the thundering approach of the race horses, Musick eased his gun out of his holster. There was shouting and cheering all around him as the horses came into sight. It would be a close finish between two horses, but Musick didn't know that. He was watching Seely, who was standing on the edge of the finish line.

In seconds the horses flashed by and the first gunshot blasted out. Musick moved toward Seely, halted, raised his gun hip high and shot Seely in the back.

Musick didn't wait to watch Seely pitch face

down. He turned, in the act of holstering his gun, and bumped into a man. He moved to go around the man, but the man moved in front of him.

Only then did Musick look at the man who held a gun pointed at him.

"I saw it," Jim said. "Drop it!"

Musick reacted as any cornered animal would. His gun was in his hand. He started to lift it and Jim fired. Musick was dead before his back hit the ground.

The turmoil that followed was slow to grow. With the gunfire and the shouting, most bettors were arguing about which horse won. Since Seely was not in sight, except to those kneeling beside him, most of the bettors assumed he had gone to the tent to pay off the winner.

Hobe was approaching Jim when the word spread. He skirted Musick's body, hauled up before Jim and asked, "He the one?"

"I shot him. Now get the hell away from me quick."

Hobe went past him toward the tent. Already people were coming up to Musick's body, connecting the two shootings. Jim moved a short distance away and when he was asked a question played the dumb Indian and only shrugged in answer.

It wasn't long before Sheriff Inglish and his fat deputy came down the race course, riding so fast it scattered the curious who were crossing the track.

Jim watched while the sheriff observed the body and tried to find witnesses. Inevitably, a couple of men pointed to Musick's body and the sheriff walked up to it. He and his deputy turned over the body and found nothing but some money in the pockets.

Baffled, the sheriff looked up and saw Jim on the edge of the crowd. He said something to his deputy, who headed back toward Seely's body.

The sheriff walked around Musick's body, came up to Jim, and halted. "Know anything about this, Byers?"

"Everything," Jim said. "Let's go where we can talk."

Jim led the way out of the crowd, heading toward the tent. Hobe fell in beside them and the sheriff only nodded.

Behind the tent Jim halted and the three men faced each other.

"First," Jim said, "I killed the man you just looked over."

"Why?"

"Because he was going to kill me. I saw him shoot Seely and told him I did."

"Who is he?" Inglish asked.

"I don't know."

The sheriff looked at Hobe, "Do *you* know?"

Hobe shook his head in negation. "Never saw him before."

Before Inglish could reach for a new question Jim asked, "How do you get two dead men into town?"

"We always bring a wagon for the drunks or the hurt riders. Why?"

"Mind stoppin' at a boardin' house on the way to the hardware store? It might help with the man none of us know."

The sheriff nodded. In a matter of minutes the spring wagon, driven by Deputy Humbolt and bearing the bodies of Seely and Musick, passed them, and the sheriff caught up with it. He talked with his deputy, then signaled Jim to move up and lead the way. Hobe joined him and they led the way to Stacey's boarding house.

There, Jim dismounted and went inside. He came out ahead of Anna and Stacey. The sheriff was dismounted and waiting, as was Hobe. He knew Jim well enough to guess what this was all about, but he kept silent.

Jim halted by the sheriff and waited until the women joined them. "You all know each other," he said, and to Stacey, "Girl, you don't have to look at this. It wouldn't mean anything to you. But it would to Anna. When I pull this blanket back off the dead man, tell us if you've ever seen him, Anna. Get up on the stepping block."

Anna did and Jim moved over to the closed wagon and whipped back the blanket from Musick's heavy body, which was face up.

Anna made no grimace of revulsion, no

178

sound either. She said quietly, "That's the man who shot the two LS hands here. He's the man. He signed in as John Smith."

"He's not from around here," the sheriff said to her. "What grudge did he have against Seely and LS? Seely is the other dead man under the canvas."

"Want me to make a guess?" Hobe put in. At the sheriff's nod, Hobe told him his hunch. "Seely hired John Smith to shoot the two LS hands, only his name isn't John Smith."

"Then what is his name?" Inglish demanded.

"I don't know. John Smith is his 'summer name.'"

"What's that mean, 'summer name'?"

"That's when the law wants him somewhere under his right name."

"So you think Seely hired him to shoot two of his men. Why?"

Jim said, "To put the blame on Hobe. Don't the peace bond sworn out on Hobe prove it?"

"But why would Smith shoot the man that paid him?" the sheriff asked, and added, "That is, if your guess is right, and it don't have to be."

Hobe said, "Because Seely was the only man who knew he shot those two men here. With Seely dead there wouldn't be anything pointing to him."

"I won't buy it," the sheriff said.

"All right," Hobe said. "Send your deputy back to the races. Once they're done there'll be an unclaimed horse tied up or walking around. Once you've got the brand and check it out in other counties it might tell you something."

"Do that, Ed," the sheriff said to his deputy. "Deliver the bodies and get back here." The deputy drove off and the sheriff eyed Jim. "If you were close enough to this Smith to gun him down you were close enough to stop him from shootin' Seely."

"It was Hobe I was watchin' for, nobody else."

The sheriff shook his head in disgust and moved toward his horse. Jim and Hobe tied their horses to the hitching post and joined the waiting women.

Jim and Anna headed up the walk for the house. Stacey put her arm in Hobe's and they, too, headed for the house.

"Being a woman, I suppose you'll want a church wedding?"

Stacey hugged his arm. "I don't care if it's held in the barn. Just so it happens."

Ⓧ - 5 - 19 - 09